THE
ROMANCE
OF THE
MILKY
WAY
&
OTHER
STUDIES
AND
STORIES

THE RO-MANCE OF THE MILKY ❂ WAY

AND OTHER STUDIES ⅋ STORIES BY LAFCADIO HEARN ❂

Short Story Index Reprint Series

BOOKS FOR LIBRARIES PRESS
FREEPORT, NEW YORK

First published 1905
Reprinted 1969

Standard Book Number: 8369-3004-5

LIBRARY OF CONGRESS CATALOG CARD NUMBER:

77-75779

CONTENTS

LAFCADIO HEARN, known to Nippon
as Yakumo Koizumi, was born in Leucadia in
the Ionian Islands, June 27, 1850. His father
was an Irish surgeon in the British Army ; his
mother was a Greek. Both parents died while
Hearn was still a child, and he was adopted by
a great-aunt, and educated for the priesthood.
To this training he owed his Latin scholarship
and, doubtless, something of the subtlety of his
intelligence. He soon found, however, that the
prospect of an ecclesiastical career was alien from
his inquiring mind and vivid temperament, and
at the age of nineteen he came to America to
seek his fortune. After working for a time as a
proof-reader, he obtained employment as a newspaper reporter in Cincinnati. Soon he rose to
be an editorial writer, and went in the course of
a few years to New Orleans to join the editorial
staff of the " Times-Democrat." Here he lived
until 1887, writing odd fantasies and arabesques
for his paper, contributing articles and sketches

to the magazines, and publishing several curious little books, among them his " Stray Leaves from Strange Literature," and his translations from Gautier. In the winter of 1887 he began his pilgrimages to exotic countries, being, as he wrote to a friend, " a small literary bee in search of inspiring honey." After a couple of years, spent chiefly in the French West Indies, with periods of literary work in New York, he went in 1890 to Japan to prepare a series of articles for a magazine. Here through some deep affinity of mood with the marvelous people of that country he seems suddenly to have felt himself at last at home. He married a Japanese woman; he acquired Japanese citizenship in order to preserve the succession of his property to his family there; he became a lecturer in the Imperial University at Tōkyō; and in a series of remarkable books he made himself the interpreter to the Western World of the very spirit of Japanese life and art. He died there of paralysis of the heart on the 26th of September, 1904.

With the exception of a body of familiar letters now in process of collection, the present volume contains all of Hearn's writing that he left uncollected in the magazines or in manuscript of a sufficient ripeness for publication. It is worth noting, however, that perfect as is the writing of "Ultimate Questions," and complete as the essay is in itself, the author regarded it as unfinished, and, had he lived, would have revised and amplified some portions of it.

But if this volume lacks the incomparably exquisite touch of its author in its arrangement and revision, it does, nevertheless, present him in all of his most characteristic veins, and it is in respect both to style and to substance perhaps the most mature and significant of his works.

In his first days as a writer Hearn had conceived an ideal of his art as specific as it was ambitious. Early in the eighties he wrote from New Orleans in an unpublished letter to the Rev. Wayland D. Ball of Washington : "The lovers of antique loveliness are proving to me the future possibilities of a long cherished dream, — the English realization of a Latin style, modeled upon foreign masters, and rendered even more forcible by that element of *strength* which is the characteristic of Northern tongues. This no man can hope to accomplish, but even a translator may carry his stones to the master-masons of a new architecture of language." In the realization of his ideal Hearn took unremitting pains. He gave a minute and analytical study to the writings of such masters of style as Flaubert and Gautier, and he chose his miscellaneous reading with a peculiar care. He wrote again to the same friend : " I never read a book which does not powerfully impress the imagination ; but whatever contains novel, curious, potent imagery I always read, no matter what the subject. When the soil of fancy is really well enriched with innumerable fallen leaves, the flowers of language grow spontaneously." Finally, to the hard study of technique, to vast but judicious reading, he added a long, creative brooding time. To a Japanese friend, Nobushige Amenomori, he wrote in a passage which contains by implication a deep theory not only of literary composition, but of all art : —

" Now with regard to your own sketch or story. If you are quite dissatisfied with it, I think this is probably due *not* to what you suppose, — imperfection of expression, — but rather to the fact that some *latent* thought or emotion has not yet defined itself in

your mind with sufficient sharpness. You feel
something and have not been able to express the
feeling — only because you do not yet quite
know what it is. We feel without understanding feeling; and our most powerful emotions
are the most undefinable. This must be so, because they are inherited accumulations of feeling, and the multiplicity of them — superimposed
one over another — blurs them, and makes them
dim, even though enormously increasing their
strength. . . . *Unconscious* brain work is the
best to develop such latent feeling or thought.
By quietly writing the thing over and over again,
I find that the emotion or idea often *develops
itself* in the process, — unconsciously. Again,
it is often worth while to *try* to analyze the feeling that remains dim. The effort of trying to
understand exactly what it is that moves us
sometimes proves successful. . . . If you have
any feeling — no matter what — strongly latent
in the mind (even only a haunting sadness or
a mysterious joy), you may be sure that it is
expressible. Some feelings are, of course, very
difficult to develop. I shall show you one of
these days, when we see each other, a page that
I worked at for *months* before the idea came
clearly. . . . When the best result comes, it

ought to surprise you, for our best work is out of the Unconscious."

Through this study, reading, and brooding Lafcadio Hearn's prose ripened and mellowed consistently to the end. In mere workmanship the present volume is one of his most admirable, while in its heightened passages, like the final paragraph of "The Romance of the Milky Way," the rich, melancholy music, the profound suggestion, are not easily matched from any but the very greatest English prose.

In substance the volume is equally significant. In 1884 he wrote to one of the closest of his friends that he had at last found his feet intellectually through the reading of Herbert Spencer which had dispelled all "isms" from his mind and left him "the vague but omnipotent consolation of the Great Doubt." And in "Ultimate Questions," which strikes, so to say, the dominant chord of this volume, we have an almost lyrical expression of the meaning for him of the Spencerian philosophy and psychology. In it is his characteristic mingling of Buddhist and Shintō thought with English and French psychology, strains which in his work "do not simply mix well," as he says in one of his letters, but "absolutely unite, like chemical ele-

xii

ments, — rush together with a shock;" — and in it he strikes his deepest note. In his steady envisagement of the horror that envelops the stupendous universe of science, in his power to evoke and revive old myths and superstitions, and by their glamour to cast a ghostly light of vanished suns over the darkness of the abyss, he was the most Lucretian of modern writers.

In outward appearance Hearn, the man, was in no way prepossessing. In the sharply lined picture of him drawn by one of his Japanese comrades in the "Atlantic" for October, 1905, he appears, "slightly corpulent in later years, short in stature, hardly five feet high, of somewhat stooping gait. A little brownish in complexion, and of rather hairy skin. A thin, sharp, aquiline nose, large protruding eyes, of which the left was blind and the right very near-sighted."

The same writer, Nobushige Amenomori, has set down a reminiscence, not of Hearn the man, but of Hearn the genius, wherewith this introduction to the last of his writings may fitly conclude: "I shall ever retain the vivid remembrance of the sight I had when I stayed over night at his house for the first time. Being used myself also to sit up late, I read in bed that night. The clock struck one in the morning, but there was a light in Hearn's study. I heard some low, hoarse coughing. I was afraid my friend might be ill; so I stepped out of my room and went to his study. Not wanting, however, to disturb him, if he was at work, I cautiously opened the door just a little, and peeped in. I saw my friend intent in writing at his high desk, with his nose almost touching the paper. Leaf after leaf he wrote on. In a while he held up his head, and what did I see! It was not the Hearn I was familiar with; it was another Hearn. His face was mysteriously white; his large eye gleamed. He appeared like one in touch with some unearthly presence.

"Within that homely looking man there burned something pure as the vestal fire, and in that flame dwelt a mind that called forth life and poetry out of dust, and grasped the highest themes of human thought."

F. G.

September, 1905.

THE
ROMANCE
OF THE
MILKY
WAY

Of old it was said : ' The River of Heaven is the Ghost of Waters.' We behold it shifting its bed in the course of the year as an earthly river sometimes does.

Ancient Scholar

THE
ROMANCE
OF
THE
MILKY
WAY

Among the many charming festivals celebrated by Old Japan, the most romantic was the festival of Tanabata-Sama, the Weaving-Lady of the Milky Way. In the chief cities her holiday is now little observed; and in Tōkyō it is almost forgotten. But in many country districts, and even in villages near the capital, it is still celebrated in a small way. If you happen to visit an old-fashioned country town or village, on the seventh day of the seventh month (by the ancient calendar), you will probably notice many freshly-cut bamboos fixed upon the roofs of the houses, or planted in the ground beside them, every bamboo having attached to it a number of strips of colored

3

paper. In some very poor villages you might find that these papers are white, or of one color only ; but the general rule is that the papers should be of five or seven different colors. Blue, green, red, yellow, and white are the tints commonly displayed. All these papers are inscribed with short poems written in praise of Tanabata and her husband Hikoboshi. After the festival the bamboos are taken down and thrown into the nearest stream, together with the poems attached to them.

To understand the romance of this old festival, you must know the legend of those astral divinities to whom offerings used to be made, even by the Imperial Household, on the seventh day of the seventh month. The legend is Chinese. This is the Japanese popular version of it : —

The great god of the firmament had a lovely daughter, Tanabata-tsumé, who passed her days in weaving garments for her august parent. She rejoiced in her work, and thought that there was no greater pleasure than the

4

pleasure of weaving. But one day, as she sat
before her loom at the door of her heavenly
dwelling, she saw a handsome peasant lad pass
by, leading an ox, and she fell in love with him.
Her august father, divining her secret wish,
gave her the youth for a husband. But the
wedded lovers became too fond of each other,
and neglected their duty to the god of the
firmament; the sound of the shuttle was no
longer heard, and the ox wandered, unheeded,
over the plains of heaven. Therefore the great
god was displeased, and he separated the pair.
They were sentenced to live thereafter apart,
with the Celestial River between them; but it
was permitted them to see each other once a
year, on the seventh night of the seventh moon.
On that night — providing the skies be clear
— the birds of heaven make, with their bodies
and wings, a bridge over the stream; and by
means of that bridge the lovers can meet. But
if there be rain, the River of Heaven rises, and
becomes so wide that the bridge cannot be
formed. So the husband and wife cannot always
meet, even on the seventh night of the seventh

month; it may happen, by reason of bad weather, that they cannot meet for three or four years at a time. But their love remains immortally young and eternally patient; and they continue to fulfill their respective duties each day without fault, — happy in their hope of being able to meet on the seventh night of the next seventh month.

To ancient Chinese fancy, the Milky Way was a luminous river, — the River of Heaven, — the Silver Stream. It has been stated by Western writers that Tanabata, the Weaving-Lady, is a star in Lyra; and the Herdsman, her beloved, a star in Aquila, on the opposite side of the galaxy. But it were more correct to say that both are represented, to Far-Eastern imagination, by groups of stars. An old Japanese book puts the matter thus plainly: "Kengyū (the Ox-Leader) is on the west side of the Heavenly River, and is represented by three stars in a row, and looks like a man leading an ox. Shokujo (the Weaving-Lady) is on the east side of the Heavenly River: three stars

6

so placed as to appear like the figure of a wo-man seated at her loom. . . . The former pre-sides over all things relating to agriculture; the latter, over all that relates to women's work."

In an old book called Zatsuwa-Shin, it is said that these deities were of earthly origin. Once in this world they were man and wife, and lived in China; and the husband was called Is-shi, and the wife Hakuyō. They especially and most devoutly reverenced the Moon. Every clear evening, after sundown, they waited with eagerness to see her rise. And when she began to sink towards the horizon, they would climb to the top of a hill near their house, so that they might be able to gaze upon her face as long as possible. Then, when she at last disap-peared from view, they would mourn together. At the age of ninety and nine, the wife died; and her spirit rode up to heaven on a magpie, and there became a star. The husband, who was then one hundred and three years old, sought consolation for his bereavement in look-ing at the Moon; and when he welcomed her rising and mourned her setting, it seemed to him as if his wife were still beside him.

One summer night, Hakuyō — now immortally beautiful and young — descended from heaven upon her magpie, to visit her husband; and he was made very happy by that visit. But from that time he could think of nothing but the bliss of becoming a star, and joining Hakuyō beyond the River of Heaven. At last he also ascended to the sky, riding upon a crow; and there he became a star-god. But he could not join Hakuyō at once, as he had hoped; — for between his allotted place and hers flowed the River of Heaven; and it was not permitted for either star to cross the stream, because the Master of Heaven (*Ten-Tei*) daily bathed in its waters. Moreover, there was no bridge. But on one day every year — the seventh day of the seventh month — they were allowed to see each other. The Master of Heaven goes always on that day to the Zenhōdo, to hear the preaching of the law of Buddha; and then the magpies and the crows make, with their hovering bodies and outspread wings, a bridge over the

8

Celestial Stream; and Hakuyō crosses that bridge to meet her husband.

There can be little doubt that the Japanese festival called Tanabata was originally identical with the festival of the Chinese Weaving-Goddess, Tchi-Niu; the Japanese holiday seems to have been especially a woman's holiday, from the earliest times; and the characters with which the word Tanabata is written signify a weaving-girl. But as both of the star-deities were worshiped on the seventh of the seventh month, some Japanese scholars have not been satisfied with the common explanation of the name, and have stated that it was originally composed with the word *tané* (seed, or grain), and the word *hata* (loom). Those who accept this etymology make the appellation, Tanabata-Sama, plural instead of singular, and render it as "the deities of grain and of the loom," — that is to say, those presiding over agriculture and weaving. In old Japanese pictures the star-gods are represented according to this conception of their respective attributes; — Hikoboshi being figured as a peasant lad

9

leading an ox to drink of the Heavenly River, on the farther side of which Orihimé (Tanabata) appears, weaving at her loom. The garb of both is Chinese; and the first Japanese pictures of these divinities were probably copied from some Chinese original.

In the oldest collection of Japanese poetry extant, — the Manyōshū, dating from 760 A. D., — the male divinity is usually called Hikoboshi, and the female Tanabata-tsumé; but in later times both have been called Tanabata. In Izumo the male deity is popularly termed O-Tanabata Sama, and the female Mé-Tanabata Sama. Both are still known by many names. The male is called Kaiboshi as well as Hikoboshi and Kengyū; while the female is called Asagao-himé ("Morning Glory Princess"),[1] Ito-ori-himé ("Thread-Weaving Princess"), Momoko-himé ("Peach-Child Princess"), Takimono-himé ("Incense Princess"), and Sasagani-himé ("Spider Princess"). Some of these names are difficult to explain, —

[1] Asagao (lit., "morning-face") is the Japanese name for the beautiful climbing plant which we call "morning glory."

especially the last, which reminds us of the Greek legend of Arachne. Probably the Greek myth and the Chinese story have nothing whatever in common; but in old Chinese books there is recorded a curious fact which might well suggest a relationship. In the time of the Chinese Emperor Ming Hwang (whom the Japanese call Gensō), it was customary for the ladies of the court, on the seventh day of the seventh month, to catch spiders and put them into an incense-box for purposes of divination. On the morning of the eighth day the box was opened; and if the spiders had spun thick webs during the night the omen was good. But if they had remained idle the omen was bad.

There is a story that, many ages ago, a beautiful woman visited the dwelling of a farmer in the mountains of Izumo, and taught to the only daughter of the household an art of weaving never before known. One evening the beautiful stranger vanished away; and the people knew that they had seen the Weaving-Lady of Heaven. The daughter of the farmer became renowned for her skill in weaving. But she would never marry, — because she had been the companion of Tanabata-Sama.

Then there is a Chinese story — delightfully vague — about a man who once made a visit, unawares, to the Heavenly Land. He had observed that every year, during the eighth month, a raft of precious wood came floating to the shore on which he lived; and he wanted to know where that wood grew. So he loaded a boat with provisions for a two years' voyage, and sailed away in the direction from which the rafts used to drift. For months and months he sailed on, over an always placid sea; and at last he arrived at a pleasant shore, where wonderful trees were growing. He moored his boat, and proceeded alone into the unknown land, until he came to the bank of a river whose waters were bright as silver. On the opposite shore he saw a pavilion; and in the pavilion a beautiful woman sat weaving; she was white like moonshine, and made a radiance all about her. Presently he saw a handsome young pea-

sant approaching, leading an ox to the water;
and he asked the young peasant to tell him the
name of the place and the country. But the
youth seemed to be displeased by the question,
and answered in a severe tone: "If you want
to know the name of this place, go back to
where you came from, and ask Gen-Kum-Pei." [1]
So the voyager, feeling afraid, hastened to his
boat, and returned to China. There he sought
out the sage Gen-Kum-Pei, to whom he related
the adventure. Gen-Kum-Pei clapped his hands
for wonder, and exclaimed, "So it was you!
. . . On the seventh day of the seventh month
I was gazing at the heavens, and I saw that
the Herdsman and the Weaver were about to
meet;—but between them was a new Star,
which I took to be a Guest-Star. Fortunate
man! you have been to the River of Heaven,
and have looked upon the face of the Weaving-
Lady! . . . "

—It is said that the meeting of the
Herdsman and the Weaver can be observed by

[1] This is the Japanese reading of the Chinese name.

any one with good eyes; for whenever it occurs those stars burn with five different colors. That is why offerings of five colors are made to the Tanabata divinities, and why the poems composed in their praise are written upon paper of five different tints.

But, as I have said before, the pair can meet only in fair weather. If there be the least rain upon the seventh night, the River of Heaven will rise, and the lovers must wait another whole year. Therefore the rain that happens to fall on Tanabata night is called *Namida no Amé*, "The Rain of Tears."

When the sky is clear on the seventh night, the lovers are fortunate; and their stars can be seen to sparkle with delight. If the star Kengyū then shines very brightly, there will be great rice crops in the autumn. If the star Shokujo looks brighter than usual, there will be a prosperous time for weavers, and for every kind of female industry.

In old Japan it was generally supposed that the meeting of the pair signified

14

good fortune to mortals. Even to-day, in many parts of the country, children sing a little song on the evening of the Tanabata festival, — *Tenki ni nari!* ("O weather, be clear!") In the province of Iga the young folks also sing a jesting song at the supposed hour of the lovers' meeting : —

> Tanabata ya!
> Amari isogaba,
> Korobubéshi! [1]

But in the province of Izumo, which is a very rainy district, the contrary belief prevails; and it is thought that if the sky be clear on the seventh day of the seventh month, misfortune will follow. The local explanation of this belief is that if the stars can meet, there will be born from their union many evil deities who will afflict the country with drought and other calamities.

[1] "Ho! Tanabata! if you hurry too much, you will tumble down!"

The festival of Tanabata was first celebrated in Japan on the seventh day of the seventh month of Tembyō Shōhō (A. D. 755). Perhaps the Chinese origin of the Tanabata divinities accounts for the fact that their public worship was at no time represented by many temples.

I have been able to find record of only one temple to them, called Tanabata-jinja, which was situated at a village called Hoshiai-mura, in the province of Owari, and surrounded by a grove called Tanabata-mori.[1]

Even before Tembyō Shōhō, however, the legend of the Weaving-Maiden seems to have been well known in Japan; for it is recorded that on the seventh night of the seventh year of Yōrō (A. D. 723) the poet Yamagami no Okura composed the song: —

Amanogawa,
Ai-muki tachité,
Waga koïshi

[1] There is no mention, however, of any such village in any modern directory.

Kimi kimasu nari —
Himo-toki makina ! [1]

It would seem that the Tanabata festival was first established in Japan eleven hundred and fifty years ago, as an Imperial Court festival only, in accordance with Chinese precedent. Subsequently the nobility and the military classes everywhere followed imperial example; and the custom of celebrating the Hoshi-matsuri, or Star-Festival, — as it was popularly called, — spread gradually downwards, until at last the seventh day of the seventh month became, in the full sense of the term, a national holiday. But the fashion of its observance varied considerably at different eras and in different provinces.

The ceremonies at the Imperial Court were of the most elaborate character: a full account of them is given in the *Kōji Kongen*, — with explanatory illustrations. On the evening of the seventh day of the seventh month, mat-

[1] For a translation and explanation of this song, see *infra*, page 30.

tings were laid down on the east side of that portion of the Imperial Palace called the Seiryōden; and upon these mattings were placed four tables of offerings to the Star-deities. Besides the customary food-offerings, there were placed upon these tables rice-wine, incense, vases of red lacquer containing flowers, a harp and flute, and a needle with five eyes, threaded with threads of five different colors. Black-lacquered oil-lamps were placed beside the tables, to illuminate the feast. In another part of the grounds a tub of water was so placed as to reflect the light of the Tanabata-stars; and the ladies of the Imperial Household attempted to thread a needle by the reflection. She who succeeded was to be fortunate during the following year.

The court-nobility (*Kugé*) were obliged to make certain offerings to the Imperial House on the day of the festival. The character of these offerings, and the manner of their presentation, were fixed by decree. They were conveyed to the palace upon a tray, by a veiled lady of rank, in ceremonial dress. Above her, as she walked, a great red umbrella was borne

18

by an attendant. On the tray were placed seven *tanzaku* (longilateral slips of fine tinted paper for the writing of poems) ; seven *kudzu*-leaves ; [1] seven inkstones ; seven strings of *sōmen* (a kind of vermicelli) ; fourteen writing-brushes ; and a bunch of yam-leaves gathered at night, and thickly sprinkled with dew. In the palace grounds the ceremony began at the Hour of the Tiger, — 4 A. M. Then the inkstones were carefully washed, — prior to preparing the ink for the writing of poems in praise of the Star-deities, — and each one set upon a *kudzu*-leaf. One bunch of bedewed yam-leaves was then laid upon every inkstone ; and with this dew, instead of water, the writing-ink was prepared. All the ceremonies appear to have been copied from those in vogue at the Chinese court in the time of the Emperor Ming-Hwang.

It was not until the time of the Toku-gawa Shōgunate that the Tanabata festival be-came really a national holiday ; and the popular custom of attaching *tanzaku* of different colors

[1] *Pueraria Thunbergiana.*

to freshly-cut bamboos, in celebration of the occasion, dates only from the era of Bunsei (1818). Previously the *tanzaku* had been made of a very costly quality of paper; and the old aristocratic ceremonies had been not less expensive than elaborate. But in the time of the Tokugawa Shōgunate a very cheap paper of various colors was manufactured; and the holiday ceremonies were suffered to assume an inexpensive form, in which even the poorest classes could indulge.

The popular customs relating to the festival differed according to locality. Those of Izumo — where all classes of society, *samurai* or common folk, celebrated the holiday in much the same way — used to be particularly interesting; and a brief account of them will suggest something of the happy aspects of life in feudal times. At the Hour of the Tiger, on the seventh night of the seventh month, everybody was up; and the work of washing the inkstones and writing-brushes was performed. Then, in the household garden, dew was collected upon yam-leaves. This dew was called *Amanogawa no suzuki*

20

("drops from the River of Heaven"); and it was used to make fresh ink for writing the poems which were to be suspended to bamboos planted in the garden. It was usual for friends to present each other with new inkstones at the time of the Tanabata festival; and if there were any new inkstones in the house, the fresh ink was prepared in these. Each member of the family then wrote poems. The adults composed verses, according to their ability, in praise of the Star-deities; and the children either wrote dictation or tried to improvise. Little folk too young to use the writing-brush without help had their small hands guided, by parent or elder sister or elder brother, so as to shape on a *tanzaku* the character of some single word or phrase relating to the festival, — such as "Amanogawa," or "Tanabata," or "Kasasagi no Hashi" (the Bridge of Magpies). In the garden were planted two freshly-cut bamboos, with branches and leaves entire, — a male bamboo (*otoko-daké*) and a female bamboo (*onna-daké*). They were set up about six feet apart, and to a cord extended between them were suspended paper-cuttings of five colors, and skeins of dyed thread of five colors. The paper-cuttings represented upper-robes,—*kimono*. To the leaves and branches of the bamboos were tied the *tanzaku* on which poems had been written by the members of the family. And upon a table, set between the bamboos, or immediately before them, were placed vessels containing various offerings to the Star-deities,—fruits, *sōmen*, rice-wine, and vegetables of different kinds, such as cucumbers and watermelons.

But the most curious Izumo custom relating to the festival was the *Nému-nagashi*, or "Sleep-wash-away" ceremony. Before daybreak the young folks used to go to some stream, carrying with them bunches composed of *némuri*-leaves and bean-leaves mixed together. On reaching the stream, they would fling their bunches of leaves into the current, and sing a little song : —

> Nému wa, nagaré yo !
> Mamé no ha wa, tomaré !

These verses might be rendered in two ways;

because the word *nému* can be taken in the meaning either of *némuri* (sleep), or of *nemuri-gi* or *némunoki*, the "sleep-plant" (mimosa), — while the syllables *mamé*, as written in *kana*, can signify either "bean," or "activity," or "strength," "vigor," "health," etc. But the ceremony was symbolical, and the intended meaning of the song was : —

> Drowsiness, drift away !
> Leaves of vigor, remain !

After this, all the young folk would jump into the water, to bathe or swim, in token of their resolve to shed all laziness for the coming year, and to maintain a vigorous spirit of endeavor.

Yet it was probably in Yédo (now Tōkyō) that the Tanabata festival assumed its most picturesque aspects. During the two days that the celebration lasted, — the sixth and seventh of the seventh month, — the city used to present the appearance of one vast bamboo grove ; fresh bamboos, with poems attached to them, being erected upon the roofs of the

23

houses. Peasants were in those days able to do a great business in bamboos, which were brought into town by hundreds of wagonloads for holiday use. Another feature of the Yédo festival was the children's procession, in which bamboos, with poems attached to them, were carried about the city. To each such bamboo there was also fastened a red plaque on which were painted, in Chinese characters, the names of the Tanabata stars.

But almost everywhere, under the Tokugawa régime, the Tanabata festival used to be a merry holiday for the young people of all classes, — a holiday beginning with lantern displays before sunrise, and lasting well into the following night. Boys and girls on that day were dressed in their best, and paid visits of ceremony to friends and neighbors.

— The moon of the seventh month used to be called *Tanabata-tsuki*, or "The Moon of Tanabata." And it was also called *Fumi-tsuki*, or "The Literary Moon," because during the seventh month poems were everywhere composed in praise of the Celestial Lovers.

❈

❈   ❈

I think that my readers ought to be interested in the following selection of ancient Japanese poems, treating of the Tanabata legend. All are from the *Manyōshū*. The *Manyōshū*, or " Gathering of a Myriad Leaves," is a vast collection of poems composed before the middle of the eighth century. It was compiled by Imperial order, and completed early in the ninth century. The number of the poems which it contains is upwards of four thousand; some being "long poems " (*naga-uta*), but the great majority *tanka*, or compositions limited to thirty-one syllables; and the authors were courtiers or high officials. The first eleven *tanka* hereafter translated were composed by Yamagami no Okura, Governor of the province of Chikuzen more than eleven hundred years ago. His fame as a poet is well deserved ; for not a little of his work will bear comparison with some of the finer epigrams of the Greek Anthology. The following verses, upon the death of his little son Furubi, will serve as an example : —

> Wakakeréba
> Nichi-yuki shiraji :
> Mahi wa sému,
> Shitabé no tsukahi
> Ohité-tohorasé.

— [*As he is so young, he cannot know the way. . . . To the messenger of the Underworld I will give a bribe, and entreat him, saying : " Do thou kindly take the little one upon thy back along the road."*]

Eight hundred years earlier, the Greek poet Diodorus Zonas of Sardis had written : —

" *Do thou, who rowest the boat of the dead in the water of this reedy lake, for Hades, stretch out thy hand, dark Charon, to the son of Kinyras, as he mounts the ladder by the gangway, and receive him. For his sandals will cause the lad to slip, and he fears to set his feet naked on the sand of the shore.*"

26

But the charming epigram of Diodorus was inspired only by a myth, — for the "son of Kinyras" was no other than Adonis, — whereas the verses of Okura express for us the yearning of a father's heart.

— Though the legend of Tanabata was indeed borrowed from China, the reader will find nothing Chinese in the following compositions. They represent the old classic poetry at its purest, free from alien influence ; and they offer us many suggestions as to the condition of Japanese life and thought twelve hundred years ago. Remembering that they were written before any modern European literature had yet taken form, one is startled to find how little the Japanese written language has changed in the course of so many centuries. Allowing for a few obsolete words, and sundry slight changes of pronunciation, the ordinary Japanese reader to-day can enjoy these early productions of his native muse with about as little difficulty as the English reader finds in studying the poets of the Elizabethan era. Moreover, the refinement and the simple charm of the *Manyōshū* compositions have never been surpassed, and seldom equaled, by later Japanese poets.

As for the forty-odd *tanka* which I have translated, their chief attraction lies, I think, in what they reveal to us of the human nature of their authors. Tanabata-tsumé still represents for us the Japanese wife, worshipfully loving; — Hikoboshi appears to us with none of the luminosity of the god, but as the young Japanese husband of the sixth or seventh century, before Chinese ethical convention had begun to exercise its restraints upon life and literature. Also these poems interest us by their expression of the early feeling for natural beauty. In them we find the scenery and the seasons of Japan transported to the Blue Plain of High Heaven; — the Celestial Stream with its rapids and shallows, its sudden risings and clamorings within its stony bed, and its water-grasses bending in the autumn wind, might well be the Kamo-gawa; — and the mists that haunt its shores are the very mists of Arashiyama. The boat of Hikoboshi, impelled by a single oar working upon a

28

wooden peg, is not yet obsolete; and at many a
country ferry you may still see the *hiki-funé* in
which Tanabata-tsumé prayed her husband to
cross in a night of storm, — a flat broad barge
pulled over the river by cables. And maids and
wives still sit at their doors in country villages,
on pleasant autumn days, to weave as Tanabata-
tsumé wove for the sake of her lord and lover.

— It will be observed that, in most of
these verses, it is not the wife who dutifully
crosses the Celestial River to meet her husband,
but the husband who rows over the stream to
meet the wife; and there is no reference to
the Bridge of Birds. . . . As for my renderings, those readers who know by experience
the difficulty of translating Japanese verse will
be the most indulgent, I fancy. The Romaji
system of spelling has been followed (except
in one or two cases where I thought it better
to indicate the ancient syllabication after the
method adopted by Aston); and words or
phrases necessarily supplied have been inclosed
in parentheses.

Amanogawa
Ai-muki tachité,
Waga koïshi
Kimi kimasu nari
Himo-toki makéna !

    [*He is coming, my long-desired lord, whom I have been waiting to meet here, on the banks of the River of Heaven. . . . The moment of loosening my girdle is nigh !* [1]]

Hisakata no [2]
Ama no kawasé ni,
Funé ukété,
Koyoï ka kimi ga
Agari kimasan ?

[1] The last line alludes to a charming custom of which mention is made in the most ancient Japanese literature. Lovers, ere parting, were wont to tie each other's inner girdle (*himo*) and pledge themselves to leave the knot untouched until the time of their next meeting. This poem is said to have been composed in the seventh year of Yōrō, — A. D. 723, — eleven hundred and eighty-two years ago.

[2] *Hisakata-no* is a "pillow-word" used by the old poets in relation to celestial objects ; and it is often difficult to translate. Mr. Aston thinks that the literal meaning of *hisakata* is simply "long-hard," in the sense of long-enduring, — *hisa*

[*Over the Rapids of the Everlasting Heaven, floating in his boat, my lord will doubtless deign to come to me this very night.*]

Kazé kumo wa
Futatsu no kishi ni
Kayoëdomo,
Waga toho-tsuma no
Koto zo kayowanu !

[*Though winds and clouds to either bank may freely come or go, between myself and my far-away spouse no message whatever may pass.*]

Tsubuté [1] ni mo
Nagé koshitsu-béki,
Amanogawa
Hédatéréba ka mo,
Amata subé-naki !

(long), *katai* (hard, or firm),—so that *hisakata-no* would have the meaning of "firmamental." Japanese commentators, however, say that the term is composed with the three words, *hi* (sun), *sasu* (shine), and *kata* (side) ;—and this etymology would justify the rendering of *hisakata-no* by some such expression as "light-shedding," "radiance-giving." On the subject of pillow-words, see Aston's *Grammar of the Japanese Written Language*.

[1] The old text has *tabuté*.

[*To the opposite bank one might easily fling a pebble; yet, being separated from him by the River of Heaven, alas! to hope for a meeting (except in autumn) is utterly useless.*]

Aki-kazé no
Fukinishi hi yori
" Itsushika " to — ;
Waga machi koïshi
Kimi zo kimaséru.

[*From the day that the autumn wind began to blow (I kept saying to myself), "Ah! when shall we meet?" — but now my beloved, for whom I waited and longed, has come indeed!*]

Amanogawa
Ito kawa-nami wa
Tatanédomo,
Samorai gatashi —
Chikaki kono sé wo.

[*Though the waters of the River of Heaven have not greatly risen, (yet to cross) this near stream and to wait upon (my lord and lover) remains impossible.*]

32

Sodé furaba
Mi mo kawashitsu-béku
Chika-kerédo,
Wataru subé nashi,
Aki nishi aranéba.

[*Though she is so near that the waving
of her (long) sleeves can be distinctly seen, yet there is
no way to cross the stream before the season of autumn.*]

Kagéroï no
Honoka ni miété
Wakarénaba ; —
Motonaya koïn
Aü-toki madé wa !

[*When we were separated, I had seen
her for a moment only, — and dimly as one sees a fly-
ing midge;* [1] *now I must vainly long for her as before,
until time of our next meeting !*]

Hikoboshi no
Tsuma mukaë-buné
Kogizurashi, —
Ama-no-Kawara ni
Kiri no tatéru wa.

[1] *Kagéroï* is an obsolete form of *kagérō*, meaning an
ephemera.

[*Methinks that Hikoboshi must be rowing his boat to meet his wife, — for a mist (as of oar-spray) is rising over the course of the Heavenly Stream.*]

Kasumi tatsu
Ama-no-Kawara ni,
Kimi matsu to, —
Ikayō hodo ni
Mono-suso nurenu.

[*While awaiting my lord on the misty shore of the River of Heaven, the skirts of my robe have somehow become wet.*]

Amanogawa,
Mi-tsu no nami oto
Sawagu-nari :
Waga matsu-kimi no
Funadé-surashi mo.

[*On the River of Heaven, at the place of the august ferry, the sound of the water has become loud : perhaps my long-awaited lord will soon be coming in his boat.*]

Tanabata no
Sodé maku yoï no
Akatoki wa,
Kawasé no tazu wa
Nakazu to mo yoshi.

[*As Tanabata (slumbers) with her long
sleeves rolled up, until the reddening of the dawn, do
not, O storks of the river-shallows, awaken her by
your cries.*[1]]

Amanogawa
Kiri-tachi-wataru :
Kyō, kyō, to —
Waga matsu-koïshi
Funadé-surashi !

[(*She sees that*) *a mist is spreading across
the River of Heaven*. . . . " *To-day, to-day,*" *she thinks,
" my long-awaited lord will probably come over in his
boat.*"]

Amanogawa,
Yasu no watari ni,
Funé ukété ; —

[1] Lit., " not to cry out (will be) good " — but a literal
translation of the poem is scarcely possible.

Waga tachi-matsu to
Imo ni tsugé koso.

[*By the ferry of Yasu, on the River of
Heaven, the boat is floating: I pray you tell my
younger sister* [1] *that I stand here and wait.*]

Ō-sora yo
Kayō waré sura,
Na ga yué ni,
Amanokawa-ji no
Nazumité zo koshi.

[*Though I (being a Star-god) can pass
freely to and fro, through the great sky, — yet to cross
over the River of Heaven, for your sake, was weary
work indeed!*]

Yachihoko no
Kamî no mi-yo yori
Tomoshi-zuma ; —
Hito-shiri ni keri
Tsugitéshi omoëba.

[1] That is to say, " wife." In archaic Japanese the word
imo signified both " wife " and " younger sister." The term
might also be rendered " darling." or " beloved."

36

[From the august Age of the God-of-Eight-Thousand-Spears,[1] she had been my spouse in secret[2] only ; yet now, because of my constant longing for her, our relation has become known to men.]

Amé tsuchi to
Wakaréshi toki yo
Onoga tsuma ;
Shika zo té ni aru
Aki matsu aré wa.

[From the time when heaven and earth were parted, she has been my own wife ; — yet, to be with her, I must always wait till autumn.[3]]

Waga kōru
Niho no omo wa

[1] Yachihoko-no-Kami, who has many other names, is the Great God of Izumo, and is commonly known by his appellation Oho-kuni-nushi-no-Kami, or the " Deity-Master-of-the Great-Land." He is locally worshiped also as the god of marriage, — for which reason, perhaps, the poet thus refers to him.

[2] Or, "my seldom-visited spouse." The word *tsuma* (*zuma*), in ancient Japanese, signified either wife or husband ; and this poem might be rendered so as to express either the wife's or the husband's thoughts.

[3] By the ancient calendar, the seventh day of the seventh month would fall in the autumn season.

Koyoï mo ka
Ama-no-kawara ni
Ishi-makura makan.

[*With my beloved, of the ruddy-tinted
cheeks,*[1] *this night indeed will I descend into the bed of
the River of Heaven, to sleep on a pillow of stone.*]

Amanogawa.
Mikomori-gusa no
Aki-kazé ni
Nabikafu miréba,
Toki kitarurashi.

[*When I see the water-grasses of the River
of Heaven bend in the autumn wind (I think to myself)* : " *The time (for our meeting) seems to have
come.*"]

Waga séko ni
Ura-koi oréba,
Amanogawa
Yo-funé kogi-toyomu
Kaji no 'to kikoyu.

[1] The literal meaning is " *béni*-tinted face," — that is to
say, a face of which the cheeks and lips have been tinted with
béni, a kind of rouge.

38

[When I feel in my heart a sudden long-ing for my husband,[1] then on the River of Heaven the sound of the rowing of the night-boat is heard, and the plash of the oar resounds.]

Tō-zuma to
Tamakura kawashi
Nétaru yo wa,
Tori-gané na naki
Akéba aku to mo!

[In the night when I am reposing with my (now) far-away spouse, having exchanged jewel-pillows[2] with her, let not the cock crow, even though the day should dawn.]

Yorozu-yo ni
Tazusawari ité
Ai mi-domo,

---

[1] In ancient Japanese the word *séko* signified either husband or elder brother. The beginning of the poem might also be rendered thus:— " When I feel a secret longing for my husband," etc.

[2] " To exchange jewel-pillows " signifies to use each other's arms for pillows. This poetical phrase is often used in the earliest Japanese literature. The word for jewel, *tama*, often appears in compounds as an equivalent of "precious," " dear," etc.

Omoi-sugu-béki
Koi naranaku ni.

[*Though for a myriad ages we should remain hand-in-hand and face to face, our exceeding love could never come to an end. (Why then should Heaven deem it necessary to part us?)*]

Waga tamé to,
Tanabata-tsumé no,
Sono yado ni,
Oréru shirotai
Nuït ken kamo?

[*The white cloth which Tanabata has woven for my sake, in that dwelling of hers, is now, I think, being made into a robe for me.*]

Shirakumo no
I-ho é kakurité
Tō-kédomo,
Yoï-sarazu min
Imo ga atari wa.

[*Though she be far-away, and hidden from me by five hundred layers of white cloud, still shall I turn my gaze each night toward the dwelling-place of my younger sister (wife).*]

40

Aki saréba
Kawagiri tatéru
Amanogawa,
Kawa ni muki-ité
Kru [1] yo zo ōki!

[*When autumn comes, and the river-mists
spread over the Heavenly Stream, I turn toward the
river, (and long) ; and the nights of my longing are
many !*]

Hito-tosé ni
Nanuka no yo nomi
Aü-hito no —
Koï mo tsuki-néba
Sayo zo aké ni keru!

[*But once in the whole year, and only
upon the seventh night (of the seventh month), to meet
the beloved person — and lo! The day has dawned
before our mutual love could express itself!* [2]]

Toshi no koï
Koyoï tsukushíté,
Asu yori wa,

[1] For *kofuru.*
[2] Or "satisfy itself." A literal rendering is difficult.

41

Tsuné no gotoku ya
Waga koï oran.

[*The love-longing of one whole year having ended to-night, every day from to-morrow I must
again pine for him as before!*]

Hikoboshi to
Tanabata-tsumé to
Koyoï aü ; —
Ama-no-Kawa to ni
Nami tatsu-na yumé!

[*Hikoboshi and Tanabata-tsumé are to
meet each other to-night; — ye waves of the River of
Heaven, take heed that ye do not rise!*]

Aki-kazé no
Fuki tadayowasu
Shirakumo wa,
Tanabata-tsumé no
Amatsu hiré kamo?

[*Oh! that white cloud driven by the
autumn-wind — can it be the heavenly* hiré [1] *of Tanabata-tsumé?*]

[1] At different times, in the history of Japanese female

42

Shiba-shiba mo
Ai minu kimi wo,
Amanogawa
Funa-dé haya séyo
Yo no fukénu ma ni.

[*Because he is my not-often-to-be-met beloved, hasten to row the boat across the River of
Heaven ere the night be advanced.*]

Amanogawa
Kiri tachi-watari
Hikoboshi no
Kaji no 'to kikoyu
Yo no fuké-yukéba.

[*Late in the night, a mist spreads over*

costume, different articles of dress were called by this name.
In the present instance, the *hiré* referred to was probably a
white scarf, worn about the neck and carried over the shoul-
ders to the breast, where its ends were either allowed to hang
loose, or were tied into an ornamental knot. The *hiré* was
often used to make signals with, much as handkerchiefs are
waved to-day for the same purpose; — and the question
uttered in the poem seems to signify : " Can that be Tanabata waving her scarf — to call me ? " In very early times,
the ordinary costumes worn were white.

43

the River of Heaven; and the sound of the oar [1] *of Hikoboshi is heard.*]

Amanogawa
Kawa 'to sayakéshi :
Hikoboshi no
Haya kogu funé no
Nami no sawagi ka ?

[*On the River of Heaven a sound of plashing can be distinctly heard: is it the sound of the rippling made by Hikoboshi quickly rowing his boat ?*]

Kono yūbé,
Furikuru amé wa,
Hikoboshi no
Haya kogu funé no
Kaï no chiri ka mo.

[*Perhaps this evening shower is but the spray (flung down) from the oar of Hikoboshi, rowing his boat in haste.*]

[1] Or, "the creaking of the oar." (The word *kaji* to-day means "helm"; — the single oar, or scull, working upon a pivot, and serving at once for rudder and oar, being now called *ro*.) The mist passing across the Amanogawa is, according to commentators, the spray from the Star-god's oar.

44

Waga tama-doko wo
Asu yori wa
Uchi haraï,
Kimi to inézuté
Hitori ka mo nen!

[*From to-morrow, alas! after having put my jewel-bed in order, no longer reposing with my lord, I must sleep alone!*]

Kazé fukité,
Kawa-nami tachinu; —
Hiki-funé ni
Watari mo kimasé
Yo no fukénu ma ni.

[*The wind having risen, the waves of the river have become high; — this night cross over in a towboat,[1] I pray thee, before the hour be late!*]

Amanogawa
Nami wa tatsutomo,
Waga funé wa
Iza kogi iden
Yo no fukénu ma ni.

[*Even though the waves of the River of*

---

[1] Lit. "pull-boat" (*hiki-funé*), — a barge or boat pulled by a rope.

Heaven run high, I must row over quickly, before it becomes late in the night.]

Inishié ni
Oritéshi hata wo ;
Kono yūbé
Koromo ni nuïté —
Kimi matsu aré wo !

[*Long ago I finished weaving the material ; and, this evening, having finished sewing the garment for him — (why must) I still wait for my lord ?*]

Amanogawa
Sé wo hayami ka mo ?
Nubatama no
Yo wa fuké ni tsutsu,
Awanu Hikoboshi !

[*Is it that the current of the River of*

---

[1] *Nubatama no yo* might better be rendered by some such phrase as " the berry-black night," — but the intended effect would be thus lost in translation. *Nubatama-no* (a " pillow-word ") is written with characters signifying " like the black fruits of *Karasu-Ōgi ; *" and the ancient phrase " *nubatama no yo* " therefore may be said to have the same meaning as our expressions " jet-black night," or " pitch-dark night."

Heaven (has become too) rapid? The jet-black night advances — and Hikoboshi has not come!]

Watashi-mori,
Funé haya watasé; —
Hito-tosé ni
Futatabi kayō
Kimi naranaku ni!

[*Oh, ferryman, make speed across the stream! — my lord is not one who can come and go twice in a year!*]

Aki kazé no
Fukinishi hi yori,
Amanogawa
Kawasé ni dédachi; —
Matsu to tsugé koso!

[*On the very day that the autumn-wind began to blow, I set out for the shallows of the River of Heaven; — I pray you, tell my lord that I am waiting here still!*]

Tanabata no
Funanori surashi, —
Maso-kagami,

47

Kiyoki tsuki-yo ni
Kumo tachi-wataru.

[Methinks Tanabata must be coming in her boat ; for a cloud is even now passing across the clear face of the moon.[1]]

— And yet it has been gravely asserted that the old Japanese poets could find no beauty in starry skies ! . . .

Perhaps the legend of Tanabata, as it was understood by those old poets, can make but a faint appeal to Western minds. Nevertheless, in the silence of transparent nights, before the rising of the moon, the charm of the ancient tale sometimes descends upon me, out of the scintillant sky, — to make me forget the monstrous facts of science, and the stupendous horror of Space. Then I no longer behold the Milky Way as that awful Ring of the Cosmos,

---

[1] Composed by the famous poet Ōtomo no Sukuné Ya-kamochi, while gazing at the Milky Way, on the seventh night of the seventh month of the tenth year of Tampyō (A. D. 738). The pillow-word in the third line (*maso-kagami*) is untranslatable.

48

whose hundred million suns are powerless to
lighten the Abyss, but as the very Amanogawa
itself, — the River Celestial. I see the thrill of
its shining stream, and the mists that hover
along its verge, and the water-grasses that bend
in the winds of autumn. White Orihimé I see
at her starry loom, and the Ox that grazes on
the farther shore ; — and I know that the falling dew is the spray from the Herdsman's oar.
And the heaven seems very near and warm
and human ; and the silence about me is filled
with the dream of a love unchanging, immortal,
— forever yearning and forever young, and forever left unsatisfied by the paternal wisdom of
the gods.

GOBLIN
POETRY

GOBLIN
POETRY

RECENTLY, while groping about an old book shop, I found a collection of Goblin Poetry in three volumes, containing many pictures of goblins. The title of the collection is *Kyōka Hyaku-Monogatari,* or "The Mad Poetry of the *Hyaku-Monogatari.*" The *Hyaku-Monogatari,* or "Hundred Tales," is a famous book of ghost stories. On the subject of each of the stories, poems were composed at different times by various persons, — poems of the sort called *Kyōka,* or Mad Poetry, — and these were collected and edited to form the three volumes of which I became the fortunate possessor. The collecting was done by a certain Takumi Jingorō, who wrote under the literary pseudonym "Temméï Réōjin" (Ancient of the Temméï Era). Takumi died in the first year of Bunkyū (1861), at the good age of eighty ; and his collection seems to have been published in the sixth year of Kaéï (1853). The pictures were made by an artist called Masazumi, who worked under the pseudonym " Ryōsai Kanjin."

From a prefatory note it appears that Takumi Jingorō published his collection with the hope of reviving interest in a once popular kind of poetry which had fallen into neglect before the middle of the century. The word *kyōka* is written with a Chinese character signifying " insane " or " crazy ; " and it means a particular and extraordinary variety of comic poetry. The form is that of the classic *tanka* of thirty-one syllables (arranged 57577) ; — but the subjects are always the extreme reverse of classical; and the artistic effects depend upon methods of verbal jugglery which cannot be explained without the help of numerous examples. The collection published by Takumi includes a good deal of matter in which a Western reader can discover no merit ; but the

54

best of it has a distinctly grotesque quality
that reminds one of Hood's weird cleverness in
playing with grim subjects. This quality, and
the peculiar Japanese method of mingling the
playful with the terrific, can be suggested and
explained only by reproducing in Romaji the
texts of various *kyōka*, with translations and
notes.

The selection which I have made
should prove interesting, not merely because it
will introduce the reader to a class of Japanese
poetry about which little or nothing has yet
been written in English, but much more because it will afford some glimpses of a supernatural world which still remains for the most
part unexplored. Without knowledge of Far
Eastern superstitions and folk-tales, no real
understanding of Japanese fiction or drama or
poetry will ever become possible.

There are many hundreds of poems in
the three volumes of the *Kyōka Hyaku-Monogatari ;* but the number of the ghosts and goblins falls short of the one hundred suggested by

55

the title. There are just ninety-five. I could not expect to interest my readers in the whole of this goblinry, and my selection includes less than one seventh of the subjects. The Faceless Babe, The Long-Tongued Maiden, The Three-Eyed Monk, The Pillow-Mover, The Thousand Heads, The Acolyte-with-the-Lantern, The Stone-that-Cries-in-the-Night, The Goblin-Heron, The Goblin-Wind, The Dragon-Lights, and The Mountain-Nurse, did not much impress me. I omitted *kyōka* dealing with fancies too gruesome for Western nerves, — such as that of the *Obumédori*, — also those treating of merely local tradition. The subjects chosen represent national rather than provincial folklore, — old beliefs (mostly of Chinese origin) once prevalent throughout the country, and often referred to in its popular literature.

I. KITSUNÉ–BI

The Will-o'-the-wisp is called *kitsuné-bi* (" fox-fire "), because the goblin-fox was formerly supposed to create it. In old Japanese

56

pictures it is represented as a tongue of pale red flame, hovering in darkness, and shedding no radiance upon the surfaces over which it glides.

To understand some of the following *kyōka* on the subject, the reader should know that certain superstitions about the magical power of the fox have given rise to several queer folk-sayings, — one of which relates to marrying a stranger. Formerly a good citizen was expected to marry within his own community, not outside of it; and the man who dared to ignore traditional custom in this regard would have found it difficult to appease the communal indignation. Even to-day the villager who, after a long absence from his birthplace, returns with a strange bride, is likely to hear unpleasant things said, — such as: "*Wakaranai-mono wo hippaté-kita! . . . Doko no uma no honé da ka?*" ("Goodness knows what kind of a thing he has dragged here after him! Where did he pick up that old horse-bone?") The expression *uma no honé*, "old horse-bone," requires explanation.

57

A goblin-fox has the power to assume many shapes; but, for the purpose of deceiving *men*, he usually takes the form of a pretty woman. When he wants to create a charming phantom of this kind, he picks up an old horse-bone or cow-bone, and holds it in his mouth. Presently the bone becomes luminous; and the figure of a woman defines about it, — the figure of a courtesan or singing-girl. . . . So the village query about the man who marries a strange wife, " What old horse-bone has he picked up ? " signifies really, " What wanton has bewitched him ? " It further implies the suspicion that the stranger may be of outcast blood : a certain class of women of pleasure having been chiefly recruited, from ancient time, among the daughters of Éta and other pariah-people.

Hi tomoshité
Kitsuné no kwaséshi,
Asobimé [1] wa —

[1] *Asobimé*, a courtesan : lit., " sporting-woman." The Éta and other pariah classes furnished a large proportion of these women. The whole meaning of the poem is as follows: " See that young wanton with her lantern ! It is a pretty

Izuka no uma no
Honé ni ya aruran !

[— *Ah the wanton* (*lighting her lantern*) *!
— so a fox-fire is kindled in the time of fox-transfor-
mation! . . . Perhaps she is really nothing more
than an old horse-bone from somewhere or other. . . .*]

Kitsuné-bi no
Moyuru ni tsukété,
Waga tama no
Kiyuru yō nari
Kokoro-hoso-michi !

[*Because of that Fox-fire burning there,
the very soul of me is like to be extinguished in this
narrow path* (*or, in this heart-depressing solitude*).[1]]

sight — but so is the sight of a fox, when the creature kin-
dles his goblin-fire and assumes the shape of a girl. And
just as your fox-woman will prove to be no more than an
old horse-bone, so that young courtesan, whose beauty de-
ludes men to folly, may be nothing better than an Éta."

[1] The supposed utterance of a belated traveler frightened
by a will-o'-the-wisp. The last line allows of two readings.
Kokoro-hosoi means "timid;" and *hosoi michi* (*hoso-michi*)
means a "narrow path," and, by implication, a "lonesome
path."

59

II. RIKOMBYŌ

The term *Rikombyō* is composed with the word *rikon*, signifying a "shade," "ghost," or "spectre," and the word *byō*, signifying "sickness," "disease." An almost literal rendering would be "ghost-sickness." In Japanese-English dictionaries you will find the meaning of *Rikombyō* given as "hypochondria;" and doctors really use the term in this modern sense. But the ancient meaning was *a disorder of the mind which produced a Double;* and there is a whole strange literature about this weird disease. It used to be supposed, both in China and Japan, that under the influence of intense grief or longing, caused by love, the spirit of the suffering person would create a Double. Thus the victim of *Rikombyō* would appear to have two bodies, exactly alike; and one of these bodies would go to join the absent beloved, while the other remained at home. (In my "Exotics and Retrospectives," under the title "A Question in the Zen Texts," the reader will find a typical

Chinese story on the subject, — the story of
the girl Ts'ing.) Some form of the primitive
belief in doubles and wraiths probably exists in
every part of the world ; but this Far Eastern
variety is of peculiar interest because the double
is supposed to be caused by love, and the subjects of the affliction to belong to the gentler
sex. . . . The term *Rikombyō* seems to be applied to the apparition as well as to the mental
disorder supposed to produce the apparition : it
signifies " doppelgänger " as well as " ghost-dis-
ease."

— With these necessary explanations,
the quality of the following *kyōka* can be understood. A picture which appears in the
Kyōka Hyaku-Monogatari shows a maid-servant
anxious to offer a cup of tea to her mistress,
— a victim of the " ghost-sickness." The servant cannot distinguish between the original
and the apparitional shapes before her ; and
the difficulties of the situation are suggested
in the first of the *kyōka* which I have translated : —

Ko-ya, soré to?
Ayamé mo wakanu
Rikombyō:
Izuré wo tsuma to
Hiku zo wazuraü!

[*Which one is this? — which one is that?
Between the two shapes of the Rikombyō it is not possible to distinguish. To find out which is the real wife
— that will be an affliction of spirit indeed!*]

Futatsu naki
Inochi nagara mo
Kakégaë no
Karada no miyuru —
Kagé no wazurai!

[*Two lives there certainly are not; — nevertheless an extra body is visible, by reason of the
Shadow-Sickness.*]

Naga-tabi no
Oto wo shitaïté
Mi futatsu ni
Naru wa onna no
Sāru rikombyō.

[*Yearning after her far-journeying hus-band, the woman has thus become two bodies, by reason of her ghostly sickness.*]

Miru kagé mo
Naki wazurai no
Rikombyō, —
Omoi no hoka ni
Futatsu miru kagé !

[*Though (it was said that), because of her ghostly sickness, there was not even a shadow of her left to be seen, — yet, contrary to expectation, there are two shadows of her to be seen !* [1]]

Rikombyō
Hito ni kakushité
Oku-zashiki,

[1] The Japanese say of a person greatly emaciated by sickness, *miru-kagé mo naki*: " Even a visible shadow of him is not ! " — Another rendering is made possible by the fact that the same expression is used in the sense of " unfit to be seen, — "though the face of the person afflicted with this ghostly sickness is unfit to be seen, yet by reason of her secret longing [for another man] there are now two of her faces to be seen." The phrase *omoi no hoka*, in the fourth line, means " contrary to expectation ; " but it is ingeniously made to suggest also the idea of secret longing.

63

Omoté y dëasanu
Kagé no wazurai.

*[Afflicted with the Rikombyō, she hides
away from people in the back room, and never ap-
proaches the front of the house, — because of her
Shadow-disease.[1]*

Mi wa koko ni ;
Tama wa otoko ni
Soïné suru ; —
Kokoro mo shiraga
Haha ga kaihō.

*[Here her body lies ; but her soul is far
away, asleep in the arms of a man ; — and the white-
haired mother, little knowing her daughter's heart, is
nursing (only the body).[2]*

[1] There is a curious play on words in the fourth line. The
word *omoté*, meaning "the front," might, in reading, be
sounded as *omotté*, "thinking." The verses therefore might
also be thus translated : — "She keeps her real thoughts
hidden in the back part of the house, and never allows them
to be seen in the front part of the house, — because she is
suffering from the 'Shadow-Sickness' [of love]."

[2] There is a double meaning, suggested rather than expressed, in the fourth line. The word *shiraga*, "white-hair,"
suggests *shirazu*, "not knowing."

64

Tamakushigé
Futatsu no sugata
Misénuru wa,
Awasé-kagami no
Kagé no wazurai.

[*If, when seated before her toilet-stand, she sees two faces reflected in her mirror, — that might be caused by the mirror doubling itself under the influence of the Shadow-Sickness.[1]*]

III. Ō–GAMA

In the old Chinese and Japanese literature the toad is credited with supernatural

[1] There is in this poem a multiplicity of suggestion impossible to render in translation. While making her toilet, the Japanese woman uses two mirrors (*awasé-kagami*) — one of which, a hand-mirror, serves to show her the appearance of the back part of her coiffure, by reflecting it into the larger stationary mirror. But in this case of Rikombyō, the woman sees more than her face and the back of her head in the larger mirror: she sees her own double. The verses indicate that one of the mirrors may have caught the Shadow-Sickness, and doubled itself. And there is a further suggestion of the ghostly sympathy said to exist between a mirror and the soul of its possessor.

capacities, — such as the power to call down clouds, the power to make rain, the power to exhale from its mouth a magical mist which creates the most beautiful illusions. Some toads are good spirits, — friends of holy men ; and in Japanese art a famous Rishi called "Gama-Sen-nin" (Toad Rishi) is usually represented with a white toad resting upon his shoulder, or squatting beside him. Some toads are evil goblins, and create phantasms for the purpose of luring men to destruction. A typical story about a creature of this class will be found in my "Kottō," entitled "The Story of Chūgorō."

> Mé wa kagami,
> Kuchi wa tarai no
> Hodo ni aku :
> Gama mo késhō no
> Mono to koso shiré.

[*The eye of it, widely open, like a (round) mirror; the mouth of it opening like a wash-basin — by these things you may know that the Toad is a goblin-thing (or, that the Toad is a toilet article).*[1]]

[1] There are two Japanese words, *keshō*, which in *kana* are written alike and pronounced alike, though represented by

66

IV. SHINKIRŌ

The term *Shinkirō* is used in the meaning of " mirage," and also as another name for Hōrai, the Elf-land of Far Eastern fable. Various beings in Japanese myth are credited with power to delude mortals by creating a, mirage of Hōrai. In old pictures one may see a toad represented in the act of exhaling from its mouth a vapor that shapes the apparition of Hōrai.

But the creature especially wont to produce this illusion is the *Hamaguri*, — a Japanese mollusk much resembling a clam. Opening its shell, it sends into the air a purplish misty breath ; and that mist takes form and defines, in tints of mother-of-pearl, the luminous vision of Hōrai and the palace of the Dragon-King.

Hamaguri no
Kuchi aku toki ya,

very different Chinese characters. As written in *kana*, the term *keshō-no-mono* may signify either " toilet articles " or " a monstrous being," " a goblin."

67

Shinkirō!
Yo ni shiraré ken
Tatsu-no-miya-himé!

[*When the hamaguri opens its mouth —
lo! Shinkirō appears! . . . Then all can clearly see
the Maiden-Princess of the Dragon-Palace.*]

Shinkirō —
Tatsu no miyako no
Hinagata [1] wo
Shio-hi no oki ni
Misuru hamaguri!

[*Lo! in the offing at ebb-tide, the hamaguri makes visible the miniature image of Shinkirō
— the Dragon-Capital!*]

V. ROKURO–KUBI

The etymological meaning of *Rokuro-
Kubi* can scarcely be indicated by any English
rendering. The term *rokuro* is indifferently
used to designate many revolving objects —

---

[1] *Hinagata* means especially "a model," "a miniature
copy," "a drawn plan," etc.

objects as dissimilar as a pulley, a capstan, a windlass, a turning lathe, and a potter's wheel. Such renderings of Rokuro-Kubi as "Whirling-Neck" and "Rotating-Neck" are unsatisfactory;—for the idea which the term suggests to Japanese fancy is that of a neck which revolves, *and lengthens or retracts according to the direction of the revolution.* . . . As for the ghostly meaning of the expression, a Rokuro-Kubi is either (1) a person whose neck lengthens prodigiously during sleep, so that the head can wander about in all directions, seeking what it may devour, or (2) a person able to detach his or her head completely from the body, and to rejoin it to the neck afterwards. (About this last mentioned variety of *Rokuro-Kubi* there is a curious story in my "Kwaidan," translated from the Japanese.) In Chinese mythology the being whose neck is so constructed as to allow of the head being completely detached belongs to a special class; but in Japanese folk-tale this distinction is not always maintained. One of the bad habits attributed to the Rokuro-Kubi is that of drinking the oil in night-lamps. In

69

Japanese pictures the Rokuro-Kubi is usually depicted as a woman; and old books tell us that a woman might become a Rokuro-Kubi without knowing it, — much as a somnambulist walks about while asleep, without being aware of the fact. . . . The following verses about the Rokuro-Kubi have been selected from a group of twenty in the *Kyōka Hyaku-Monogatari*: —

> Nemidaré no
> Nagaki kami woba
> Furi-wakété,
> Chi hiro ni nobasu
> Rokuro-Kubi kana!

[*Oh!* . . . *Shaking loose her long hair disheveled by sleep, the Rokuro-Kubi stretches her neck to the length of a thousand fathoms!*]

> "Atama naki
> Bakémono nari" — to
> Rokuro-Kubi,
> Mité odorokan
> Onoga karada wo.

[*Will not the Rokuro-Kubi, viewing with*

astonishment her own body (left behind) cry out, "Oh, what a headless goblin have you become!"]

Tsuka-no-ma ni
Hari wo tsutawaru,
Rokuro-Kubi
Kéta-kéta warau —
Kao no kowasa yo!

[*Swiftly gliding along the roof-beam (and among the props of the roof), the Rokuro-Kubi laughs with the sound of " kéta-kéta" — oh! the fearfulness of her face!*[1]]

Roku shaku no
Byōbu ni nobiru
Rokuro-Kubi
Mité wa, go shaku no
Mi wo chijimi-kéri!

[1] It is not possible to render all the double meanings in this composition. *Tsuka-no-ma* signifies "in a moment" or "quickly"; but it may also mean "in the space [*ma*] between the roof-props" [*tsuka*]. "*Kéta*" means a crossbeam, but *kéta-kéta warau* means to chuckle or laugh in a mocking way. Ghosts are said to laugh with the sound of kéta-kéta.

71

[*Beholding the Rokuro-Kubi rise up above the six-foot screen, any five-foot person would have become shortened by fear* (*or, " the stature of any person five feet high would have been diminished "*).*][1]

VI. YUKI–ONNA

The Snow-Woman, or Snow-Spectre, assumes various forms; but in most of the old folk-tales she appears as a beautiful phantom, whose embrace is death. (A very curious story about her can be found in my " Kwaidan.")

Yuki-Onna —
Yosō kushi mo
Atsu kōri;
Sasu-kōgai ya
Kōri naruran.

[*As for the Snow-Woman, — even her best comb, if I mistake not, is made of thick ice ; and her hair-pin,[2] too, is probably made of ice.*]

[1] The ordinary height of a full screen is six Japanese feet.

[2] *Kōgai* is the name now given to a quadrangular bar of tortoise-shell passed under the coiffure, which leaves only the ends of the bar exposed. The true hair-pin is called *kanzashi.*

72

Honrai wa
Kū naru mono ka,
Yuki-Onna?
Yoku-yoku mireba
Ichi-butsu mo nashi!

[*Was she, then, a delusion from the very first, that Snow-Woman,—a thing that vanishes into empty space? When I look carefully all about me, not one trace of her is to be seen!*]

Yo-akéréba
Kiété yuku é wa
Shirayuki [1] no
Onna to mishi mo
Yanagi nari-keri!

[*Having vanished at daybreak (that Snow-Woman), none could say whither she had gone. But what had seemed to be a snow-white woman became indeed a willow-tree!*]

[1] The term *shirayuki*, as here used, offers an example of what Japanese poets call *Kenyōgen*, or "double-purpose words." Joined to the words immediately following, it makes the phrase "white-snow woman" (*shirayuki no onna*); — united with the words immediately preceding, it suggests the reading, "whither-gone not-knowing" (*yuku é wa shira*[*zu*]).

Yuki-Onna
Mité wa yasathiku,
Matsu wo ori
Nama-daké hishigu
Chikara ari-keri!

[*Though the Snow-Woman appears to sight slender and gentle, yet, to snap the pine-trees asunder and to crush the live bamboos, she must have had strength.*]

Samukésa ni
Zotto [1] wa surédo
Yuki-Onna, —

[1] *Zotto* is a difficult word to render literally : perhaps the nearest English equivalent is " thrilling." *Zotto suru* signifies " to cause a thrill " or "to give a shock," or " to make shiver; " and of a very beautiful person it is said " *Zotto-suru hodo no bijin*," — meaning, " She is so pretty that it gives one a shock merely to look at her." The term *yanagi-goshi* (" willow-loins ") in the last line is a common expression designating a slender and graceful figure; and the reader should observe that the first half of the term is ingeniously made to do double duty here, — suggesting, with the context, not only the grace of willow branches weighed down by snow, but also the grace of a human figure that one must stop to admire, in spite of the cold.

74

Yuki oré no naki
Yanagi-goshi ka mo !

[*Though the Snow-Woman makes one shiver by her coldness, — ah, the willowy grace of her form cannot be broken by the snow* (*i. e. charms us in spite of the cold*).]

VII. FUNA–YŪRÉÏ

The spirits of the drowned are said to follow after ships, calling for a bucket or a water-dipper (*hishaku*). To refuse the bucket or the dipper is dangerous ; but the bottom of the utensil should be knocked out before the request is complied with, and the spectres must not be allowed to see this operation performed. If an undamaged bucket or dipper be thrown to the ghosts, it will be used to fill and to sink the ship. These phantoms are commonly called *Funa-Yūréï* (" Ship-Ghosts ").

The spirits of those warriors of the Héïké clan who perished in the great sea-fight at Dan-no-ura, in the year 1185, are famous among Funa-Yūréï. Taïra no Tomomori, one of the chiefs of the clan, is celebrated in this weird rôle : old pictures represent him, followed by the ghosts of his warriors, running over the waves to attack passing ships. Once he menaced a vessel in which Benkéï, the celebrated retainer of Yoshitsuné, was voyaging ; and Benkéï was able to save the ship only by means of his Buddhist rosary, which frightened the spectres away. . . .

Tomomori is frequently pictured as walking upon the sea, carrying a ship's anchor on his back. He and his fellow-ghosts are said to have been in the habit of uprooting and making off with the anchors of vessels imprudently moored in their particular domain, — the neighborhood of Shimonoséki.

Erimoto yé

Mizu kakéraruru

Kokochi seri,

" Hishaku kasé " chō

Funé no kowané ni.

[*As if the nape of our necks had been sprinkled with cold water, — so we felt while listening*

76

to the voice of the ship-ghost, saying: — " *Lend me a dipper !* " [1]]

Yūrei ni
Kasu-hishaku yori
Ichi-hayaku
Onoré ga koshi mo
Nukéru senchō.

[*The loins of the captain himself were knocked out very much more quickly than the bottom of the dipper that was to be given to the ghost.*[2]]

Benkéï no
Zuzu no kuriki ni
Tomomori no
Sugata mo ukamu —
Funé no yūréï.

[*By the virtue of Benkéï's rosary, even*

---

[1] *Hishaku*, a wooden dipper with a long handle, used to transfer water from a bucket to smaller vessels.

[2] The common expression *Koshi ga nukéru* (to have one's loins taken out) means to be unable to stand up by reason of fear. The suggestion is that while the captain was trying to knock out the bottom of a dipper, before giving it to the ghost, he fell senseless from fright.

*the ship-following ghost — even the apparition of To-
momori — is saved.*]

Yūréï wa
Ki naru Izumi no
Hito nagara,
Aö-umibara ni
Nadoté itsuran?

[*Since any ghost must be an inhabitant
of the Yellow Springs, how should a ghost appear on
the Blue Sea-Plain?* [1]]

Sono sugata,
Ikari wo ōté,
Tsuki-matoü
Funé no hésaki ya
Tomomori no réï!

[*That Shape, carrying the anchor on its
back, and following after the ship — now at the bow
and now at the stern — ah, the ghost of Tomomori.* [2]]

[1] The Underworld of the Dead — *Yomi* or Kōsen — is
called "The Yellow Springs;" these names being written
with two Chinese characters respectively signifying "yellow"
and "fountain." A very ancient term for the ocean, frequently used in the old Shintō rituals, is "The Blue Sea-
Plain."

[2] There is an untranslatable play upon words in the last

78

Tsumi fukaki
Umi ni shidzumishi,
Yūréï no
" Ukaman " toté ya !
Funé ni sugaréru.

[*Crying, " Now perchance I shall be
saved !" The ghost that sank into the deep Sea of
Sin clings to the passing ship !*[1]]

two lines. The above rendering includes two possible readings.

[1] There is more weirdness in this poem than the above
rendering suggests. The word *ukaman* in the fourth line can
be rendered as " shall perhaps float," or as " shall perhaps
be saved " (in the Buddhist sense of salvation), — as there
are two verbs *ukami.* According to an old superstition, the
spirits of the drowned must continue to dwell in the waters
until such time as they can lure the living to destruction.
When the ghost of any drowned person succeeds in drown-
ing somebody, it may be able to obtain rebirth, and to leave
the sea forever. The exclamation of the ghost in this poem
really means, " Now perhaps I shall be able to drown somebody." (A very similar superstition is said to exist on the
Breton coast.) A common Japanese saying about a child or
any person who follows another too closely and persistently
is : *Kawa de shinda-yūréï no yona tsuré-hoshigaru !* —
" Wants to follow you everywhere like the ghost of a
drowned person."

Ukaman to
Funé wo shitaëru
Yūréï wa,
Shidzumishi hito no
Omoï naruran.

[*The ghosts following after our ship in their efforts to rise again (or, "to be saved") might perhaps be the (last vengeful) thoughts of drowned men.*[1]]

Uraméshiki
Sugata wa sugoki
Yūréï no,
Kaji wo jama suru
Funé no Tomomori.

[*With vengeful aspect, the grisly ghost of Tomomori (rises) at the stern of the ship to hinder the play of her rudder.*[2]]

[1] Here I cannot attempt to render the various plays upon words; but the term "*omoï*" needs explanation. It means "thought" or "thoughts;" but in colloquial phraseology it is often used as a euphemism for a dying person's last desire of vengeance. In various dramas it has been used in the signification of "avenging ghost." Thus the exclamation, "His *thought* has come back!"—in reference to a dead man—really means: "His angry ghost appears!"

[2] There is a double meaning given by the use of the name

80

Ochi-irité,
Uwo no éjiki to
Nari ni ken ; —
Funa-yūréï mo
Nama-kusaki kazé.

[*Having perished in the sea, (those Hëïkë)
would probably have become food for fishes. (Anyhow,
whenever) the ship-following ghosts (appear), the wind
has a smell of raw fish !*[1]]

VIII. HÉÏKÉGANÌ

Readers can find in my "Kottō" a
paper about the Héïké-Crabs, which have on
their upper shells various wrinklings that resemble the outlines of an angry face. At Shimonoséki dried specimens of these curious creatures

Tomomori in the last line. *Tomo* means "the stern" of a
ship ; *mori* means "to leak." So the poem suggests that the
ghost of Tomomori not only interferes with the ship's rudder,
but causes her to leak.

[1] *Namakusaki-kaze* really means a wind having a "raw
stench ;" but the smell of bait is suggested by the second
line of the poem. A literal rendering is not possible in this
case ; the art of the composition being altogether sugges-
tive.

are offered for sale. . . . The Héïké-Crabs are said to be the transformed angry spirits of the Héïké warriors who perished at Dan-no-ura.

Shiwo-hi ni wa
Séïzoroë shité,
Héïkégani
Ukiyo no sama wo
Yoko ni niramitsu.

[*Marshaled (on the beach) at the ebb of the tide, the Héïké-crabs obliquely glare at the apparition of this miserable world.*[1]]

Saikai ni
Shizumî-nurédomo,
Héïkégani
Kōra no iro mo
Yahari aka-hata.

[*Though (the Héïké) long ago sank and perished in the Western Sea, the Héïë-crabs still dis-*

---

[1] *Hi*, the third syllable of the first line of the poem, does duty for *hi*, signifying "ebb," and for *hikata*, "dry beach." *Séïzoroë* is a noun signifying "battle-array"—in the sense of the Roman term *acies ;*—and *séïzoroé shité* means "drawn up in battle-array."

play upon their upper shells the color of the Red Standard.[1]]

Maké-ikusa
Munen to muné ni
Hasami ken ; —
Kao mo makka ni
Naru Héïkégani.

[*Because of the pain of defeat, claws have grown on their breasts, I think ; — even the faces of the Héïké-crabs have become crimson (with anger and shame).*]

Mikata mina
Oshi-tsubusaréshi
Héïkégani
Ikon wo muné ni
Hasami mochikéri.

[*All the (Héïké) party having been utterly crushed, claws have grown upon the breasts of the Héïké-crabs because of the resentment in their hearts.*[2]]

[1] The ensign of the Héïké, or Taïra clan was red; while that of their rivals, the Genji or Minamotō, was white.

[2] The use of the word *hasami* in the fifth line is a very good example of *kenyōgen*. There is a noun *hasami*, mean-

IX. YANARI

Modern dictionaries ignore the uncanny significations of the word *Yanari*, — only telling us that it means the sound of the shaking of a house during an earthquake. But the word used to mean the noise of the shaking of a house moved by a goblin; and the invisible shaker was also called *Yanari*. When, without apparent cause, some house would shudder and creak and groan in the night, folk used to suppose that it was being shaken from without by supernatural malevolence.

Tokonoma ni
Ikéshi tachiki mo
Taoré-keri ;

ing the nippers of a crab, or a pair of scissors; and there is a verb *hasami*, meaning to harbor, to cherish, or to entertain. (*Ikon wo hasamu* means "to harbor resentment against.") Reading the word only in connection with those which follow it, we have the phrase *hasami mochikéri*, " got claws ;" but, reading it with the words preceding, we have the expression *ikon wo muné ni hasami*, " resentment in their breasts nourishing."

84

Yanari ni yama no
Ugoku kakémono !

[*Even the live tree set in the alcove has
fallen down; and the mountains in the hanging picture tremble to the quaking made by the Yanari !*[1]]

X. SAKASA–BASHIRA

The term *Sakasa-bashira* (in these
kyōka often shortened into *saka-bashira*) literally means " upside-down post." A wooden post
or pillar, especially a house-post, should be set
up according to the original position of the tree
from which it was hewn, — that is to say, with
the part nearest to the roots downward. To
erect a house-post in the contrary way is thought
to be unlucky ; — formerly such a blunder was
believed to involve unpleasant consequences of
a ghostly kind, because an " upside-down " pillar would do malignant things. It would moan
and groan in the night, and move all its cracks

[1] The *tokonoma* in a Japanese room is a sort of ornamental recess or alcove, in which a picture is usually hung, and
vases of flowers, or a dwarf tree, are placed.

like mouths, and open all its knots like eyes. Moreover, the spirit of it (for every house-post has a spirit) would detach its long body from the timber, and wander about the rooms, head-downwards, making faces at people. Nor was this all. A *Sakasa-bashira* knew how to make all the affairs of a household go wrong, — how to foment domestic quarrels, — how to contrive misfortune for each of the family and the servants, — how to render existence almost insupportable until such time as the carpenter's blunder should be discovered and remedied.

Saka-bashira
Tatéshi wa tazo ya ?
Kokoro ni mo
Fushi aru hito no
Shiwaza naruran.

[*Who set the house-pillar upside-down ? Surely that must have been the work of a man with a knot in his heart.*]

Hidayama wo
Kiri-kité tatéshi
Saka-bashira —

86

Nanno takumi[1] no
Shiwaza naruran ?

[*That house-pillar hewn in the mountains of Hida, and thence brought here and erected upside-down — what carpenter's work can it be ? (or, "for what evil design can this deed have been done ? ")*]

Uë shita wo
Chigaëté tatéshi
Hashira ni wa
Sakasama-goto no
Uréï aranan.

[*As for that house-pillar mistakenly planted upside-down, it will certainly cause adversity and sorrow.*[2]]

Kabé ni mimi
Arité, kiké to ka ?
Sakashima ni

[1] The word *takumi*, as written in *kana*, may signify either "carpenter" or "intrigue," "evil plot," "wicked device." Thus two readings are possible. According to one reading, the post was fixed upside-down through inadvertence; according to the other, it was so fixed with malice prepense.

[2] Lit., "upside-down-matter-sorrow." *Sakasama-goto*, "upside-down affair," is a common expression for calamity, contrariety, adversity, vexation.

Tatéshi hashira ni
Yanari suru oto!

[*O Ears that be in the wall!* [1] *listen, will ye? to the groaning and the creaking of the house-post that was planted upside-down!*]

Uri-iyé no
Aruji wo toëba,
Oto arité:
Waré mé ga kuchi wo
Aku saka-bashira.

[*When I inquired for the master of the house that was for sale, there came to me only a strange sound by way of reply, — the sound of the upside-down house-post opening its eyes and mouth!* [2] (*i. e. its cracks*).]

[1] Alluding to the proverb, *Kabé ni mimi ari* ("There are ears in the wall"), which signifies: "Be careful how you talk about other people, even in private."

[2] There is a pun in the fourth line which suggests more than even a free translation can express. *Waré* means "I," or "mine," or "one's own," etc., according to circumstances; and *waré mé* (written separately) might be rendered "its own eyes." But *warémé* (one word) means a crack, rent, split, or fissure. The reader should remember that the term *saka-*

Omoĭkiya!
Sakasa-bashira no
Hashira-kaké
Kakinishit uta mo
Yamai ari to wa!

[*Who could have thought it! — even the poem inscribed upon the pillar-tablet, attached to the pillar which was planted upside-down, has taken the same (ghostly) sickness.*[1]]

XI. BAKÉ–JIZŌ

The figure of the Bodhi-sattva Jizō, the savior of children's ghosts, is one of the most beautiful and humane in Japanese Buddhism. Statues of this divinity may be seen in almost every village and by every roadside. But some statues of Jizō are said to do uncanny

bashira means not only "upside-down post," but also the goblin or spectre of the upside-down post.

[1] That is to say, "Even the poem on the tablet is upside-down," — all wrong. *Hashira-kaké* ("pillar-suspended thing") is the name given to a thin tablet of fine wood, inscribed or painted, which is hung to a post by way of ornament.

things — such as to walk about at night in various disguises. A statue of this kind is called a *Baké-Jizō*,[1] — meaning a Jizō that undergoes transformation. A conventional picture shows a little boy about to place the customary child's-offering of rice-cakes before the stone image of Jizō, — not suspecting that the statue moves, and is slowly bending down towards him.

> Nanigé naki
> Ishi no Jizō no
> Sugata saë,
> Yo wa osoroshiki
> Mikagé to zo naki.

[*Though the stone Jizō looks as if nothing were the matter with it, they say that at night it assumes an awful aspect (or, " Though this image appears to be a common stone Jizō, they say that at night it becomes an awful Jizō of granite."* [2])]

---

[1] Perhaps the term might be rendered "Shape-changing Jizō." The verb *bakéru* means to change shape, to undergo metamorphosis, to haunt, and many other supernatural things.

[2] The Japanese word for granite is *mikagé*; and there is also an honorific term *mikagé*, applied to divinities and em-

XII. UMI–BŌZU

Place a large cuttlefish on a table, body upwards and tentacles downwards — and you will have before you the grotesque reality that first suggested the fancy of the *Umi-Bōzu*, or Priest of the Sea. For the great bald body in this position, with the staring eyes below, bears a distorted resemblance to the shaven head of a priest ; while the crawling tentacles underneath (which are in some species united by a dark web) suggests the wavering motion of the priest's upper robe. . . . The Umi-Bōzu figures a good deal in the literature of Japanese goblinry, and in the old-fashioned picture-books. He rises from the deep in foul weather to seize his prey.

perors, which signifies " august aspect," " sacred presence," etc. . . . No literal rendering can suggest the effect, in the fifth line, of the latter reading. *Kagé* signifies " shadow," " aspect," and " power " — especially occult power ; the honorific prefix *mi*, attached to names and attributes of divinities, may be rendered " august."

Ita hitoë
Shita wa Jigoku ni,
Sumizomé no
Bōzu no umi ni
Déru mo ayashina !

[*Since there is but the thickness of a single plank (between the voyager and the sea), and underneath is Hell, 't is indeed a weird thing that a black-robed priest should rise from the sea (or, "'t is surely a marvelous happening that," etc.! [1])*]

XIII. FUDA–HÉGASHI [2]

Homes are protected from evil spirits by holy texts and charms. In any Japanese

[1] The puns are too much for me. . . . *Ayashii* means "suspicious," "marvelous," "supernatural," "weird," "doubtful."—In the first two lines there is a reference to the Buddhist proverb: *Funa-ita ichi-mai shita wa Jigoku* ("under the thickness of a single ship's-plank is Hell"). (See my *Gleanings in Buddha-Fields*, p. 206, for another reference to this saying.)

[2] *Hégashi* is the causative form of the verb *hégu*, "to pull off," "peel off," "strip off," "split off." The term *Fuda-hégashi* signifies "Make-peel-off-august-charm Ghost." In my *Ghostly Japan* the reader can find a good Japanese story about a *Fuda-hégashi*.

village, or any city by-street, you can see these texts when the sliding-doors are closed at night: they are not visible by day, when the sliding-doors have been pushed back into the *tobukuro*. Such texts are called *o-fuda* (august scripts): they are written in Chinese characters upon strips of white paper, which are attached to the door with rice-paste; and there are many kinds of them. Some are texts selected from sûtras — such as the Sûtra of Transcendent Wisdom (Pragña-Pâramitâ-Hridaya-Sûtra), or the Sûtra of the Lotos of the Good Law (Saddharma-Pundarikâ-Sûtra). Some are texts from the dhâranîs, — which are magical. Some are invocations only, indicating the Buddhist sect of the household. . . . Besides these you may see various smaller texts, or little prints, pasted above or beside windows or apertures, — some being names of Shintō gods; others, symbolical pictures only, or pictures of Buddhas and Bodhi-sattvas. All are holy charms, — *o-fuda:* they protect the houses; and no goblin or ghost can enter by night into a dwelling so protected, unless the *o-fuda* be removed.

93

Vengeful ghosts cannot themselves remove an *o-fuda;* but they will endeavor by threats or promises or bribes to make some person remove it for them. A ghost that wants to have the *o-fuda* pulled off a door is called a *Fuda-hégashi.*

Hégasan to
Rokuji-no-fuda wo,
Yuréï mo
Nam'mai dā to
Kazoëté zo miru.

[*Even the ghost that would remove the charms written with six characters actually tries to count them, repeating: "How many sheets are there?" (or, repeating, "Hail to thee, O Buddha Amitâbha!"* [1])]

[1] The fourth line gives these two readings: —

Nam'mai da? — "How many sheets are there?"
Nam [*u*] *A* [*m*]*ida!* — "Hail, O Amitâbha!"

The invocation, *Namu Amida Butsu,* is chiefly used by members of the great Shin sect; but it is also used by other sects, and especially in praying for the dead. While repeating it, the person praying numbers the utterances upon his Buddhist rosary; and this custom is suggested by the use of the word *kazoëté,* "counting."

94

Tada ichi no
Kami no o-fuda wa
Sasuga ni mo
Noriké naku to mo
Hégashi kanékéri.

[*Of the august written-charms of the god* (*which were pasted upon the walls of the house*), *not even one could by any effort be pulled off, though the rice-paste with which they had been fastened was all gone.*]

XIV. FURU–TSUBAKI

The old Japanese, like the old Greeks, had their flower-spirits and their hamadryads, concerning whom some charming stories are told. They also believed in trees inhabited by malevolent beings,— goblin trees. Among other weird trees, the beautiful *tsubaki* (*Camellia Japonica*) was said to be an unlucky tree ; — this was said, at least, of the red-flowering variety, the white-flowering kind having a better reputation and being prized as a rarity. The large fleshy crimson flowers have this curious habit : they detach themselves bodily from the

95

stem, when they begin to fade ; and they fall with an audible thud. To old Japanese fancy the falling of these heavy red flowers was like the falling of human heads under the sword ; and the dull sound of their dropping was said to be like the thud made by a severed head striking the ground. Nevertheless the tsubaki seems to have been a favorite in Japanese gardens because of the beauty of its glossy foliage ; and its flowers were used for the decoration of alcoves. But in samurai homes it was a rule never to place tsubaki-flowers in an alcove *during war-time*.

The reader will notice that in the following *kyōka* — which, as grotesques, seem to me the best in the collection — the goblin-tsubaki is called *furu-tsubaki*, "old tsubaki." The young tree was not supposed to have goblin-propensities, — these being developed only after many years. Other uncanny trees — such as the willow and the *énoki* — were likewise said to become dangerous only as they became old ; and a similar belief prevailed on the subject of uncanny animals, such as the cat — innocent in kittenhood, but devilish in age.

96

Yo-arashi ni
Chishiho itadaku
Furu tsubaki,
Hota-hota ochiru
Hana no nama-kubi.

[*When by the night-storm is shaken the
blood-crowned and ancient tsubaki-tree, then one by
one fall the gory heads of the flowers, (with the sound
of)* hota-hota !¹]

Kusa mo ki mo
Némuréru koro no
Sayo kazé ni,
Méhana no ugoku
Furu-tsubaki kana !

[*When even the grass and the trees are
sleeping under the faint wind of the night, — then do
the eyes and the noses of the old tsubaki-tree (or " the
buds and the flowers of the old tsubaki-tree ") move !* ²]

¹ The word *furu* in the third line is made to do double
duty, — as the adjective, *furu*[*i*], "ancient"; and as the
verb *furu*, "to shake." The old term *nama-kubi* (lit., " raw
head ") means a human head, freshly-severed, from which
the blood is still oozing.

² Two Japanese words are written, in *kana*, as "mé "—
one meaning " a bud ; " the other " eye." The syllables

Tomoshibi no
Kagé ayashigé ni
Miyénuru wa
Abura shiborishi
Furu-tsubaki ka-mo?

[*As for (the reason why) the light of that
lamp appears to be a Weirdness,*[1] *— perhaps the oil
was expressed from (the nuts of) the ancient tsubaki?*]

"hana," in like fashion, may signify either "flower" or
"nose." As a grotesque, this little poem is decidedly successful.

[1] *Ayashigé* is a noun formed from the adjective *ayashi*,
"suspicious," "strange," "supernatural," "doubtful." The
word *kagé* signifies both "light" and "shadow," — and is
here used with double suggestiveness. The vegetable oil
used in the old Japanese lamps used to be obtained from the
nuts of the *tsubaki*. The reader should remember that the
expression "ancient tsubaki" is equivalent to the expression
"goblin-tsubaki," — the tsubaki being supposed to turn into
a goblin-tree only when it becomes old.

98

— Nearly all the stories and folk-beliefs about which these *kyōka* were written seem to have come from China; and most of the Japanese tales of tree-spirits appear to have had a Chinese origin. As the flower-spirits and hamadryads of the Far East are as yet little known to Western readers, the following Chinese story may be found interesting.

There was a Chinese scholar — called, ın Japanese books, Tō no Busanshi— who was famous for his love of flowers. He was particularly fond of peonies, and cultivated them with great skill and patience.[1]

One day a very comely girl came to the house of Busanshi, and begged to be taken into his service. She said that circumstances obliged her to seek humble employment, but that she had received a literary education, and

[1] The tree-peony (*botan*) is here referred to, — a flower much esteemed in Japan. It is said to have been introduced· from China during the eighth century; and no less than five hundred varieties of it are now cultivated by Japanese gardeners.

therefore wished to enter, if possible, into the service of a scholar. Busanshi was charmed by her beauty, and took her into his household without further questioning. She proved to be much more than a good domestic : indeed, the nature of her accomplishments made Busanshi suspect that she had been brought up in the court of some prince, or in the palace of some great lord. She displayed a perfect knowledge of the etiquette and the polite arts which are taught only to ladies of the highest rank ; and she possessed astonishing skill in calligraphy, in painting, and in every kind of poetical composition. Busanshi presently fell in love with her, and thought only of how to please her. When scholar-friends or other visitors of importance came to the house, he would send for the new maid that she might entertain and wait upon his guests ; and all who saw her were amazed by her grace and charm.

One day Busanshi received a visit from the great Teki-Shin-Ketsu, a famous teacher of moral doctrine ; and the maid did not respond to her master's call. Busanshi went

100

himself to seek her, being desirous that Teki-Shin-Ketsu should see her and admire her ; but she was nowhere to be found. After having searched the whole house in vain, Busanshi was returning to the guest-room when he suddenly caught sight of the maid, gliding soundlessly before him along a corridor. He called to her, and hurried after her. Then she turned half-round, and flattened herself against the wall like a spider ; and as he reached her she sank backwards into the wall, so that there remained of her nothing visible but a colored shadow, — level like a picture painted on the plaster. But the shadow moved its lips and eyes, and spoke to him in a whisper, saying : —

"Pardon me that I did not obey your august call ! . . . I am not a mankind-person ; — I am only the Soul of a Peony. Because you loved peonies so much, I was able to take human shape, and to serve you. But now this Teki-Shin-Ketsu has come, — and he is a person of dreadful propriety, — and I dare not keep this form any longer. . . . I must return to the place from which I came."

Then she sank back into the wall, and vanished altogether: there was nothing where she had been except the naked plaster. And Busanshi never saw her again.

This story is written in a Chinese book which the Japanese call "Kai-ten-i-ji."

"ULTIMATE QUESTIONS"

"ULTIMATE QUESTIONS"

A MEMORY of long ago. . . . I am walking upon a granite pavement that rings like iron, between buildings of granite bathed in the light of a cloudless noon. Shadows are short and sharp : there is no stir in the hot bright air ; and the sound of my footsteps, strangely loud, is the only sound in the street. . . . Suddenly an odd feeling comes to me, with a sort of tingling shock, — a feeling, or suspicion, of universal illusion. The pavement, the bulks of hewn stone, the iron rails, and all things visible, are dreams ! Light, color, form, weight, solidity — all sensed existences — are but phantoms of being, manifestations only of one infinite ghostliness for which the language of man has not any word. . . .

This experience had been produced by study of the first volume of the Synthetic Philosophy, which an American friend had taught me how to read. I did not find it easy reading; partly because I am a slow thinker, but chiefly because my mind had never been trained to sustained effort in such directions. To learn the "First Principles" occupied me many months: no other volume of the series gave me equal trouble. I would read one section at a time, — rarely two, — never venturing upon a fresh section until I thought that I had made sure of the preceding. Very cautious and slow my progress was, like that of a man mounting, for the first time, a long series of ladders in darkness. Reaching the light at last, I caught a sudden new vision of things, — a momentary perception of the illusion of surfaces, — and from that time the world never again appeared to me quite the same as it had appeared before.

— This memory of more than twenty years ago, and the extraordinary thrill of the moment, were recently revived for me by the

reading of the essay "Ultimate Questions,"
in the last and not least precious volume be-
queathed us by the world's greatest thinker.
The essay contains his final utterance about the
riddle of life and death, as that riddle presented
itself to his vast mind in the dusk of a lifetime
of intellectual toil. Certainly the substance of
what he had to tell us might have been inferred
from the Synthetic Philosophy; but the particular interest of this last essay is made by
the writer's expression of personal sentiment
regarding the problem that troubles all deep
thinkers. Perhaps few of us could have remained satisfied with his purely scientific position. Even while fully accepting his declaration of the identity of the power that "wells up
in us under the form of consciousness" with
that Power Unknowable which shapes all things,
most disciples of the master must have longed
for some chance to ask him directly, "But how
do *you* feel in regard to the prospect of personal dissolution?" And this merely emotional
question he has answered as frankly and as
fully as any of us could have desired, — perhaps

even more frankly. "Old people," he remarks apologetically, "must have many reflections in common. Doubtless one which I have now in mind is very familiar. For years past, when watching the unfolding buds in the spring, there has arisen the thought, 'Shall I ever again see the buds unfold? Shall I ever again be awakened at dawn by the song of the thrush?' Now that the end is not likely to be long postponed, there results an increasing tendency to meditate upon ultimate questions." . . . Then he tells us that these ultimate questions — "of the How and the Why, of the Whence and the Whither" — occupy much more space in the minds of those who cannot accept the creed of Christendom, than the current conception fills in the minds of the majority of men. The enormity of the problem of existence becomes manifest only to those who have permitted themselves to think freely and widely and deeply, with all such aids to thought as exact science can furnish; and the larger the knowledge of the thinker, the more pressing and tremendous the problem appears. and the more hopelessly unanswerable. To Herbert Spencer himself it must have assumed a vastness beyond the apprehension of the average mind; and it weighed upon him more and more inexorably the nearer he approached to death. He could not avoid the conviction — plainly suggested in his magnificent Psychology and in other volumes of his great work — that there exists no rational evidence for any belief in the continuance of conscious personality after death : —

"After studying primitive beliefs, and finding that there is no origin for the idea of an after-life, save the conclusion which the savage draws, from the notion suggested by dreams, of a wandering double which comes back on awaking, and which goes away for an indefinite time at death ; — and after contemplating the inscrutable relation between brain and consciousness, and finding that we can get no evidence of the existence of the last without the activity of the first, — we seem obliged to relinquish the thought that consciousness continues after physical organization has become inactive."

In this measured utterance there is no word of hope; but there is at least a carefully stated doubt, which those who will may try to develop into the germ of a hope. The guarded phrase, " we *seem* obliged to relinquish," certainly suggests that, although in the present state of human knowledge we have no reason to believe in the perpetuity of consciousness, some larger future knowledge might help us to a less forlorn prospect. From the prospect as it now appears even this mightiest of thinkers recoiled : —

. . . "But it seems a strange and repugnant conclusion that with the cessation of consciousness at death there ceases to be any knowledge of having existed. With his last breath it becomes to each the same thing as though he had never lived.

"And then the consciousness itself — what is it during the time that it continues? And what becomes of it when it ends? We can only infer that it is a specialized and individualized form of that Infinite and Eternal Energy which transcends both our knowledge and our imagination ; and that at death its elements lapse into that Infinite and Eternal Energy whence they were derived."

— *With his last breath it becomes to each the same thing as though he had never lived?* To the individual, perhaps — surely not to the humanity made wiser and better by his labors. . . . But the world must pass away : will it thereafter be the same for the universe as if humanity had never existed ? That might depend upon the possibilities of future inter-planetary communication. . . . But the whole universe of suns and planets must also perish : thereafter will it be the same as if no intelligent life had ever toiled and suffered upon those countless worlds ? We have at least the certainty that the energies of life cannot be destroyed, and the strong probability that they will help to form another life and thought in universes yet to be evolved. . . . Nevertheless, allowing for all imagined possibilities, — granting even the likelihood of some inapprehensible relation between all past and all future condi-

tioned-being, — the tremendous question remains : What signifies the whole of apparitional
existence to the Unconditioned ? As flickers
of sheet-lightning leave no record in the night,
so in that Darkness a million billion trillion
universes might come and go, and leave no
trace of their having been.

To every aspect of the problem Herbert Spencer must have given thought; but he
has plainly declared that the human intellect,
as at present constituted, can offer no solution.
The greatest mind that this world has yet produced — the mind that systematized all human
knowledge, that revolutionized modern science,
that dissipated materialism forever, that re-
vealed to us the ghostly unity of all existence,
that reëstablished all ethics upon an immutable
and eternal foundation, — the mind that could
expound with equal lucidity, and by the same
universal formula, the history of a gnat or the
history of a sun — confessed itself, before the
Riddle of Existence, scarcely less helpless than
the mind of a child.

But for me the supreme value of this last essay is made by the fact that in its pathetic statement of uncertainties and probabilities one can discern something very much resembling a declaration of faith. Though assured that we have yet no foundation for any belief in the persistence of consciousness after the death of the brain, we are bidden to remember that the ultimate nature of consciousness remains inscrutable. Though we cannot surmise the relation of consciousness to the unseen, we are reminded that it must be considered as a manifestation of the Infinite Energy, and that its elements, if dissociated by death, will return to the timeless and measureless Source of Life. . . . Science to-day also assures us that whatever existence has been — all individual life that ever moved in animal or plant, — all feeling and thought that ever stirred in human consciousness — must have flashed self-record beyond the sphere of sentiency; and though we cannot know, we cannot help imagining that the best of such registration may be destined to perpetuity. On this latter subject, for obvious reasons, Herbert Spencer has remained silent; but the reader may ponder a remarkable paragraph in the final sixth edition of the "First Principles," — a paragraph dealing with the hypothesis that consciousness may belong to the cosmic ether. This hypothesis has not been lightly dismissed by him; and even while proving its inadequacy, he seems to intimate that it may represent imperfectly some truth yet inapprehensible by the human mind : —

"The only supposition having consistency is that that in which consciousness inheres is the all-pervading ether. This we know can be affected by molecules of matter in motion, and conversely can affect the motions of molecules;—as witness the action of light on the retina. In pursuance of this supposition we may assume that the ether, which pervades not only all space but all matter, is, under special conditions in certain parts of the nervous system, capable of being affected by the nervous changes in such way as to result in feeling, and is reciprocally capable under these conditions of affecting the nervous changes. But if we accept this explanation, we must assume that the poten-

tiality of feeling is universal, and that the evolution of feeling in the ether takes place only under the extremely complex conditions occurring in certain nervous centres. This, however, is but a semblance of an explanation, since we know not what the ether is, and since, by confession of those most capable of judging, no hypothesis that has been framed accounts for all its powers. Such an explanation may be said to do no more than symbolize the phenomena by symbols of unknown natures."
— [" First Principles," § 71 *c*, definitive edition of 1900.]

— " Inscrutable is this complex consciousness which has slowly evolved out of infantine vacuity — consciousness which, in other shapes, is manifested by animate beings at large — consciousness which, during the development of every creature, makes its appearance out of what seems unconscious matter ; *suggesting the thought that consciousness, in some rudimentary form, is omnipresent.*" [1]

— Of all modern thinkers, Spencer was perhaps the most careful to avoid giving encouragement to any hypothesis unsupported

[1] *Autobiography*, vol. ii, p. 470.

by powerful evidence. Even the simple sum of his own creed is uttered only, with due reservation, as a statement of three probabilities: that consciousness represents a specialized and individualized form of the infinite Energy; that it is dissolved by death; and that its elements then return to the source of all being. As for our mental attitude toward the infinite Mystery, his advice is plain. We must resign ourselves to the eternal law, and endeavor to vanquish our ancient inheritance of superstitious terrors, remembering that, "merciless as is the Cosmic process worked out by an Unknown Power, yet vengeance is nowhere to be found in it."[1]

In the same brief essay there is another confession of singular interest, — an acknowledgment of the terror of Space. To even the ordinary mind, the notion of infinite

[1] *Facts and Comments*, p. 201.

Space, as forced upon us by those monstrous
facts of astronomy which require no serious
study to apprehend, is terrifying ; — I mean the
mere vague idea of that everlasting Night into
which the blazing of millions of suns can bring
neither light nor warmth. But to the intellect
of Herbert Spencer the idea of Space must
have presented itself after a manner incomparably more mysterious and stupendous. The
mathematician alone will comprehend the full
significance of the paragraph dealing with the
Geometry of Position and the mystery of space-
relations, — or the startling declaration that
" even could we penetrate the mysteries of existence, there would remain still more transcendent mysteries." But Herbert Spencer tells
us that, apart from the conception of these
geometrical mysteries, the problem of naked
Space itself became for him, in the twilight of
his age, an obsession and a dismay : —

. . . " And then comes the thought of this
universal matrix itself, anteceding alike creation
or evolution, whichever be assumed, and infinitely

transcending both, alike in extent and duration ; since both, if conceived at all, must be conceived as having had beginnings, while Space had no beginning. The thought of this blank form of existence which, explored in all directions as far as imagination can reach, has, beyond that, an unexplored region compared with which the part which imagination has traversed is but infinitesimal, — the thought of a Space compared with which our immeasurable sidereal system dwindles to a point is a thought too overwhelming to be dwelt upon. Of late years the consciousness that without origin or cause infinite Space has ever existed and must ever exist, produces in me a feeling from which I shrink."

How the idea of infinite Space may affect a mind incomparably more powerful than my own, I cannot know ; — neither can I divine the nature of certain problems which the laws of space-relation present to the geometrician. But when I try to determine the cause of the horror which that idea evokes within my own feeble imagination, I am able to distinguish different elements of the emotion, — par-

118

ticular forms of terror responding to particular ideas (rational and irrational) suggested by the revelations of science. One feeling — perhaps the main element of the horror — is made by the thought of being *prisoned* forever and ever within that unutterable Viewlessness which occupies infinite Space.

Behind this feeling there is more than the thought of eternal circumscription ; — there is also the idea of being perpetually penetrated, traversed, thrilled by the Nameless ; — there is likewise the certainty that no least particle of innermost secret Self could shun the eternal touch of It ; — there is furthermore the tremendous conviction that could the Self of me rush with the swiftness of light, — with more than the swiftness of light, — beyond all galaxies, beyond durations of time so vast that Science knows no sign by which their magnitudes might be indicated, — and still flee onward, onward, downward, upward, — always, always, — never could that Self of me reach nearer to any verge, never speed farther from any centre. For, in that Silence, all vastitude and height and depth and time and direction are swallowed up : relation therein could have no meaning but for the speck of my fleeting consciousness, — atom of terror pulsating alone through atomless, soundless, nameless, illimitable potentiality.

And the idea of that potentiality awakens another quality of horror, — the horror of infinite Possibility. For this Inscrutable that pulses through substance as if substance were not at all, — so subtly that none can feel the flowing of its tides, yet so swiftly that no lifetime would suffice to count the number of the oscillations which it makes within the fraction of one second, — thrills to us out of endlessness ; — and the force of infinity dwells in its lightest tremor ; the weight of eternity presses behind its faintest shudder. To that phantom-Touch, the tinting of a blossom or the dissipation of a universe were equally facile : here it caresses the eye with the charm and illusion of color ; there it bestirs into being a cluster of giant suns. All that human mind is capable of conceiving as possible (and how much

also that human mind must forever remain incapable of conceiving?) may be wrought any-
where, everywhere, by a single tremor of that
Abyss. . . .

Is it true, as some would have us
believe, that the fear of the extinction of self
is the terror supreme? . . . For the thought
of personal perpetuity in the infinite vortex is
enough to evoke sudden trepidations that no
tongue can utter, — fugitive instants of a horror too vast to enter wholly into consciousness:
a horror that can be endured in swift black
glimpsings only. And the trust that we are one
with the Absolute — dim points of thrilling in
the abyss of It — can prove a consoling faith
only to those who find themselves obliged to
think that consciousness dissolves with the
crumbling of the brain. . . . It seems to me
that few (or none) dare to utter frankly those
stupendous doubts and fears which force mor-
tal intelligence to recoil upon itself at every
fresh attempt to pass the barrier of the Know-
able. Were that barrier unexpectedly pushed

back, — were knowledge to be suddenly and vastly expanded beyond its present limits, — perhaps we should find ourselves unable to endure the revelation. . . .

Mr. Percival Lowell's astonishing book, " Mars," sets one to thinking about the results of being able to hold communication with the habitants of an older and a wiser world, — some race of beings more highly evolved than we, both intellectually and morally, and able to interpret a thousand mysteries that still baffle our science. Perhaps, in such event, we should not find ourselves able to comprehend the methods, even could we borrow the results, of wisdom older than all our civilization by myriads or hundreds of myriads of years. But would not the sudden advent of larger knowledge from some elder planet prove for us, by reason of the present moral condition of mankind, nothing less than a catastrophe? — might it not even result in the extinction of the human species? . . .

The rule seems to be that the dissemination of dangerous higher knowledge, be-

fore the masses of a people are ethically prepared to receive it, will always be prevented by
the conservative instinct; and we have reason
to suppose (allowing for individual exceptions)
that the power to gain higher knowledge is developed only as the moral ability to profit by
such knowledge is evolved. I fancy that if the
power of holding intellectual converse with
other worlds could now serve us, we should
presently obtain it. But if, by some astonishing
chance, — as by the discovery, let us suppose,
of some method of ether-telegraphy, — this
power were prematurely acquired, its exercise
would in all probability be prohibited. . . .
Imagine, for example, what would have happened during the Middle Ages to the person
guilty of discovering means to communicate
with the people of a neighboring planet! As-
suredly that inventor and his apparatus and his
records would have been burned; every trace
and memory of his labors would have been
extirpated. Even to-day the sudden discovery
of truths unsupported by human experience,
the sudden revelation of facts totally opposed to

existing convictions, might evoke some frantic revival of superstitious terrors, — some religious panic-fury that would strangle science, and replunge the world in mental darkness for a thousand years.

THE
MIRROR
MAIDEN

THE
MIRROR
MAIDEN

In the period of the Ashikaga Shō-gunate the shrine of Ogawachi-Myōjin, at Mina-mi-Isé, fell into decay; and the daimyō of the district, the Lord Kitahataké, found himself una-ble, by reason of war and other circumstances, to provide for the reparation of the building. Then the Shintō priest in charge, Matsumura Hyōgo, sought help at Kyōto from the great daimyō Hosokawa, who was known to have influence with the Shōgun. The Lord Hosokawa received the priest kindly, and promised to speak to the Shōgun about the condition of Ogawachi-Myōjin. But he said that, in any event, a grant for the restoration of the temple could not be made without due investigation and considerable delay; and he advised Matsumura to remain in the capital while the matter was being arranged. Matsumura therefore brought his family to Kyōto, and rented a house in the old Kyōgoku quarter.

This house, although handsome and spacious, had been long unoccupied. It was said to be an unlucky house. On the northeast side of it there was a well; and several former tenants had drowned themselves in that well, without any known cause. But Matsumura, being a Shintō priest, had no fear of evil spirits; and he soon made himself very comfortable in his new home.

In the summer of that year there was a great drought. For months no rain had fallen in the Five Home-Provinces; the river-beds dried up, the wells failed; and even in the capital there was a dearth of water. But the well in Matsumura's garden remained nearly full; and the water — which was very cold and clear, with a faint bluish tinge — seemed to be supplied by a spring. During the hot season many
128

people came from all parts of the city to beg for water ; and Matsumura allowed them to draw as much as they pleased. Nevertheless the supply did not appear to be diminished.

But one morning the dead body of a young servant, who had been sent from a neighboring residence to fetch water, was found floating in the well. No cause for a suicide could be imagined ; and Matsumura, remembering many unpleasant stories about the well, began to suspect some invisible malevolence. He went to examine the well, with the intention of having a fence built around it ; and while standing there alone he was startled by a sudden motion in the water, as of something alive. The motion soon ceased ; and then he perceived, clearly reflected in the still surface, the figure of a young woman, apparently about nineteen or twenty years of age. She seemed to be occupied with her toilet : he distinctly saw her touching her lips with *béni*.[1] At first her face was visible in profile only ; but presently she turned towards him and smiled. Immediately he felt a strange shock

[1] A kind of rouge, now used only to color the lips.

at his heart, and a dizziness came upon him like the dizziness of wine, and everything became dark, except that smiling face, — white and beautiful as moonlight, and always seeming to grow more beautiful, and to be drawing him down — down — down into the darkness. But with a desperate effort he recovered his will and closed his eyes. When he opened them again, the face was gone, and the light had returned; and he found himself leaning down over the curb of the well. A moment more of that dizziness, — a moment more of that dazzling lure, — and he would never again have looked upon the sun. . . .

Returning to the house, he gave orders to his people not to approach the well under any circumstances, or allow any person to draw water from it. And the next day he had a strong fence built round the well.

About a week after the fence had been built, the long drought was broken by a great rain-storm, accompanied by wind and lightning and thunder, — thunder so tremendous

130

that the whole city shook to the rolling of it,
as if shaken by an earthquake. For three days
and three nights the downpour and the light-
nings and the thunder continued; and the
Kamogawa rose as it had never risen before,
carrying away many bridges. During the third
night of the storm, at the Hour of the Ox,
there was heard a knocking at the door of the
priest's dwelling, and the voice of a woman
pleading for admittance. But Matsumura,
warned by his experience at the well, forbade
his servants to answer the appeal. He went
himself to the entrance, and asked, —

"Who calls?"

A feminine voice responded: —

"Pardon! it is I, — Yayoi![1] . . . I
have something to say to Matsumura Sama, —
something of great moment. Please open!" . . .

Matsumura half opened the door, very
cautiously; and he saw the same beautiful face
that had smiled upon him from the well. But it
was not smiling now: it had a very sad look.

"Into my house you shall not come,"

[1] This name, though uncommon, is still in use.

the priest exclaimed. " You are not a human being, but a Well-Person. . . . Why do you thus wickedly try to delude and destroy people ? "

The Well-Person made answer in a voice musical as a tinkling of jewels (*tama-wo-korogasu-koë*) : —

" It is of that very matter that I want to speak. . . . I have never wished to injure human beings. But from ancient time a Poison-Dragon dwelt in that well. He was the Master of the Well ; and because of him the well was always full. Long ago I fell into the water there, and so became subject to him ; and he had power to make me lure people to death, in order that he might drink their blood. But now the Heavenly Ruler has commanded the Dragon to dwell hereafter in the lake called Torii-no-Iké, in the Province of Shinshū ; and the gods have decided that he shall never be allowed to return to this city. So to-night, after he had gone away, I was able to come out, to beg for your kindly help. There is now very little water in the well, because of the

132

Dragon's departure; and if you will order search to be made, my body will be found there. I pray you to save my body from the well without delay; and I shall certainly return your benevolence." . . .

So saying, she vanished into the night.

Before dawn the tempest had passed; and when the sun arose there was no trace of cloud in the pure blue sky. Matsumura sent at an early hour for well-cleaners to search the well. Then, to everybody's surprise, the well proved to be almost dry. It was easily cleaned; and at the bottom of it were found some hair-ornaments of a very ancient fashion, and a metal mirror of curious form — but no trace of any body, animal or human.

Matsumura imagined, however, that the mirror might yield some explanation of the mystery; for every such mirror is a weird thing, having a soul of its own, — and the soul of a mirror is feminine. This mirror, which seemed to be very old, was deeply crusted with scurf. But when it had been carefully cleaned,

133

by the priest's order, it proved to be of rare and costly workmanship; and there were wonderful designs upon the back of it, — also several characters. Some of the characters had become indistinguishable; but there could still be discerned part of a date, and ideographs signifying, "*third month, the third day*." Now the third month used to be termed *Yayoi* (meaning, the Month of Increase); and the third day of the third month, which is a festival day, is still called *Yayoi-no-sekku*. Remembering that the Well-Person called herself " Yayoi," Matsumura felt almost sure that his ghostly visitant had been none other than the Soul of the Mirror.

He therefore resolved to treat the mirror with all the consideration due to a Spirit. After having caused it to be carefully repolished and resilvered, he had a case of precious wood made for it, and a particular room in the house prepared to receive it. On the evening of the same day that it had been respectfully deposited in that room, Yayoi herself unexpectedly appeared before the priest as he sat alone in his study. She looked even more lovely than before ; but the light of her beauty was now soft as the light of a summer moon shining through pure white clouds. After having humbly saluted Matsumura, she said in her sweetly tinkling voice : —

"Now that you have saved me from solitude and sorrow, I have come to thank you. . . . I am indeed, as you supposed, the Spirit of the Mirror. It was in the time of the Emperor Saimei that I was first brought here from Kudara ; and I dwelt in the august residence until the time of the Emperor Saga, when I was augustly bestowed upon the Lady Kamo, Naishinnō of the Imperial Court.[1] Thereafter I became an heirloom in the House of Fujiwara, and so remained until the period of Hōgen, when I was dropped into the well. There I was left and forgotten during the years

[1] The Emperor Saimei reigned from 655 to 662 (A. D.) ; the Emperor Saga from 810 to 842. — Kudara was an ancient kingdom in southwestern Korea, frequently mentioned in early Japanese history. — A *Naishinnō* was of Imperial blood. In the ancient court-hierarchy there were twenty-five ranks or grades of noble ladies ; — that of *Naishinno* was seventh in order of precedence.

of the great war.[1] The Master of the Well [2] was a venomous Dragon, who used to live in a lake that once covered a great part of this district. After the lake had been filled in, by government order, in order that houses might be built upon the place of it, the Dragon took possession of the well; and when I fell into the well I became subject to him; and he compelled me to lure many people to their deaths. But the gods have banished him forever. . . . Now I have one more favor to beseech: I entreat that you will cause me to be offered up to the Shōgun, the Lord Yoshimasa, who by descent is related to my former possessors. Do me but this last great kindness, and it will bring you

[1] For centuries the wives of the emperors and the ladies of the Imperial Court were chosen from the Fujiwara clan. — The period called Hōgen lasted from 1156 to 1159: the war referred to is the famous war between the Taira and Minamoto clans.

[2] In old-time belief every lake or spring had its invisible guardian, supposed to sometimes take the form of a serpent or dragon. The spirit of a lake or pond was commonly spoken of as *Iké-no-Mushi*, the Master of the Lake. Here we find the title "Master" given to a dragon living in a well; but the guardian of wells is really the god Suijin.

136

good-fortune. . . . But I have also to warn you of a danger. In this house, after to-morrow, you must not stay, because it will be destroyed." . . . And with these words of warning Yayoi disappeared.

Matsumura was able to profit by this premonition. He removed his people and his belongings to another district the next day; and almost immediately afterwards another storm arose, even more violent than the first, causing a flood which swept away the house in which he had been residing.

Some time later, by favor of the Lord Hosokawa, Matsumura was enabled to obtain an audience of the Shōgun Yoshimasa, to whom he presented the mirror, together with a written account of its wonderful history. Then the prediction of the Spirit of the Mirror was fulfilled; for the Shōgun, greatly pleased with this strange gift, not only bestowed costly presents upon Matsumura, but also made an ample grant of money for the rebuilding of the Temple of Ogawachi-Myōjin.

THE
STORY
OF
ITŌ
NORISUKÉ

THE
STORY
OF
ITŌ
NORISUKÉ

In the town of Uji, in the province of Yamashiro, there lived, about six hundred years ago, a young samurai named Itō Taté-waki Norisuké, whose ancestors were of the Héïké clan. Itō was of handsome person and amiable character, a good scholar and apt at arms. But his family were poor; and he had no patron among the military nobility, — so that his prospects were small. He lived in a very quiet way, devoting himself to the study of literature, and having (says the Japanese story-teller) "only the Moon and the Wind for friends."

One autumn evening, as he was taking a solitary walk in the neighborhood of the

hill called Kotobikiyama, he happened to over-
take a young girl who was following the same
path. She was richly dressed, and seemed to be
about eleven or twelve years old. Itō greeted
her, and said, " The sun will soon be setting,
damsel, and this is rather a lonesome place.
May I ask if you have lost your way?" She
looked up at him with a bright smile, and answered deprecatingly : " Nay ! I am a *miya-dzukai*,[1] serving in this neighborhood ; and I have
only a little way to go."

By her use of the term *miya-dzukai*,
Itō knew that the girl must be in the service
of persons of rank ; and her statement surprised
him, because he had never heard of any family
of distinction residing in that vicinity. But he
only said : " I am returning to Uji, where my
home is. Perhaps you will allow me to accom-
pany you on the way, as this is a very lonesome place." She thanked him gracefully,
seeming pleased by his offer ; and they walked
on together, chatting as they went. She talked
about the weather, the flowers, the butterflies,

[1] August-residence servant.

and the birds; about a visit that she had once made to Uji, about the famous sights of the capital, where she had been born; — and the moments passed pleasantly for Itō, as he listened to her fresh prattle. Presently, at a turn in the road, they entered a hamlet, densely shadowed by a grove of young trees.

[Here I must interrupt the story to tell you that, without having actually seen them, you cannot imagine how dark some Japanese country villages remain even in the brightest and hottest weather. In the neighborhood of Tōkyō itself there are many villages of this kind. At a short distance from such a settlement you see no houses : nothing is visible but a dense grove of evergreen trees. The grove, which is usually composed of young cedars and bamboos, serves to shelter the village from storms, and also to supply timber for various purposes. So closely are the trees planted that there is no room to pass between the trunks of them : they stand straight as masts, and mingle their crests so as to form a roof that excludes

143

the sun. Each thatched cottage occupies a clear space in the plantation, the trees forming a fence about it, double the height of the building. Under the trees it is always twilight, even at high noon; and the houses, morning or evening, are half in shadow. What makes the first impression of such a village almost disquieting is, not the transparent gloom, which has a certain weird charm of its own, but the stillness. There may be fifty or a hundred dwellings; but you see nobody; and you hear no sound but the twitter of invisible birds, the occasional crowing of cocks, and the shrilling of cicadæ. Even the cicadæ, however, find these groves too dim, and sing faintly; being sun-lovers, they prefer the trees outside the village. I forgot to say that you may sometimes hear a viewless shuttle — *chaka-ton, chaka-ton;* — but that familiar sound, in the great green silence, seems an elfish happening. The reason of the hush is simply that the people are not at home. All the adults, excepting some feeble elders, have gone to the neighboring fields, the women carrying their babies on their backs; and most of the children have gone to the nearest school, perhaps not less than a mile away. Verily, in these dim hushed villages, one seems to behold the mysterious perpetuation of conditions recorded in the texts of Kwang-Tze : —

"*The ancients who had the nourishment of the world wished for nothing, and the world had enough : — they did nothing, and all things were transformed : — their stillness was abysmal, and the people were all composed.*"]

. . . The village was very dark when Itō reached it ; for the sun had set, and the after-glow made no twilight in the shadowing of the trees. "Now, kind sir," the child said, pointing to a narrow lane opening upon the main road, "I have to go this way." "Permit me, then, to see you home," Itō responded; and he turned into the lane with her, feeling rather than seeing his way. But the girl soon stopped before a small gate, dimly visible in the gloom, — a gate of trelliswork, beyond which the lights of a dwelling could be seen. "Here," she said, "is the honorable residence in which I serve.

As you have come thus far out of your way, kind sir, will you not deign to enter and to rest a while?" Itō assented. He was pleased by the informal invitation; and he wished to learn what persons of superior condition had chosen to reside in so lonesome a village. He knew that sometimes a family of rank would retire in this manner from public life, by reason of government displeasure or political trouble; and he imagined that such might be the history of the occupants of the dwelling before him. Passing the gate, which his young guide opened for him, he found himself in a large quaint garden. A miniature landscape, traversed by a winding stream, was faintly distinguishable. "Deign for one little moment to wait," the child said; "I go to announce the honorable coming;" and hurried toward the house. It was a spacious house, but seemed very old, and built in the fashion of another time. The sliding doors were not closed; but the lighted interior was concealed by a beautiful bamboo curtain extending along the gallery front. Behind it shadows were moving — shadows of women; — and suddenly

146

the music of a *koto* rippled into the night. So
light and sweet was the playing that Itō could
scarcely believe the evidence of his senses. A
slumbrous feeling of delight stole over him as
he listened, — a delight strangely mingled with
sadness. He wondered how any woman could
have learned to play thus, — wondered whether
the player could be a woman, — wondered even
whether he was hearing earthly music; for en-
chantment seemed to have entered into his blood
with the sound of it.

The soft music ceased; and almost
at the same moment Itō found the little *miya-
dzukai* beside him. "Sir," she said, "it is
requested that you will honorably enter." She
conducted him to the entrance, where he removed his sandals; and an aged woman, whom
he thought to be the *Rōjo*, or matron of the
household, came to welcome him at the threshold. The old woman then led him through
many apartments to a large and well-lighted
room in the rear of the house, and with many
respectful salutations requested him to take the

147

place of honor accorded to guests of distinction. He was surprised by the stateliness of the chamber, and the curious beauty of its decorations. Presently some maid-servants brought refreshments; and he noticed that the cups and other vessels set before him were of rare and costly workmanship, and ornamented with a design indicating the high rank of the possessor. More and more he wondered what noble person had chosen this lonely retreat, and what happening could have inspired the wish for such solitude. But the aged attendant suddenly interrupted his reflections with the question:

"Am I wrong in supposing that you are Itō Sama, of Uji, — Itō Tatéwaki Norisuké ? "

Itō bowed in assent. He had not told his name to the little *miya-dzukai*, and the manner of the inquiry startled him.

"Please do not think my question rude," continued the attendant. "An old woman like myself may ask questions without improper curiosity. When you came to the house, I thought that I knew your face; and I

148

asked your name only to clear away all doubt, before speaking of other matters. I have some thing of moment to tell you. You often pass through this village, and our young Himégimi-Sama [1] happened one morning to see you going by; and ever since that moment she has been thinking about you, day and night. Indeed, she thought so much that she became ill; and we have been very uneasy about her. For that reason I took means to find out your name and residence; and I was on the point of sending you a letter when — so unexpectedly! — you came to our gate with the little attendant. Now, to say how happy I am to see you is not possible; it seems almost too fortunate a happening to be true! Really I think that this meeting must have been brought about by the favor of Enmusubi-no-Kami, — that great God of Izumo who ties the knots of fortunate union. And now that so lucky a destiny has led you hither, perhaps you will not refuse — if there

[1] A scarcely translatable honorific title compounded of the word *himé* (princess) and *kimi* (sovereign, master or mistress, lord or lady, etc.).

be no obstacle in the way of such a union — to make happy the heart of our Himégimi-Sama?"

For the moment Itō did not know how to reply. If the old woman had spoken the truth, an extraordinary chance was being offered to him. Only a great passion could impel the daughter of a noble house to seek, of her own will, the affection of an obscure and masterless samurai, possessing neither wealth nor any sort of prospects. On the other hand, it was not in the honorable nature of the man to further his own interests by taking advantage of a feminine weakness. Moreover, the circumstances were disquietingly mysterious. Yet how to decline the proposal, so unexpectedly made, troubled him not a little. After a short silence, he replied : —

"There would be no obstacle, as I have no wife, and no betrothed, and no relation with any woman. Until now I have lived with my parents ; and the matter of my marriage was never discussed by them. You must know that I am a poor samurai, without any patron among persons of rank ; and I did not wish to marry until I could find some chance to improve my condition. As to the proposal which you have done me the very great honor to make, I can only say that I know myself yet unworthy of the notice of any noble maiden."

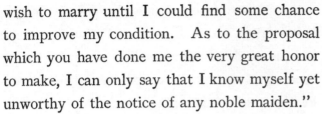

The old woman smiled as if pleased by these words, and responded : —

"Until you have seen our Himégimi-Sama, it were better that you make no decision. Perhaps you will feel no hesitation after you have seen her. Deign now to come with me, that I may present you to her."

She conducted him to another larger guest-room, where preparations for a feast had been made, and having shown him the place of honor, left him for a moment alone. She returned accompanied by the Himégimi-Sama; and, at the first sight of the young mistress, Itō felt again the strange thrill of wonder and delight that had come to him in the garden, as he listened to the music of the *koto*. Never had he dreamed of so beautiful a being. Light seemed to radiate from her presence, and to shine through her garments, as the light of the moon through flossy clouds ; her loosely flowing hair swayed about her as she moved, like the boughs of the drooping willow bestirred by the breezes of spring; her lips were like flowers of the peach besprinkled with morning dew. Itō was bewildered by the vision. He asked himself whether he was not looking upon the person of Amano-kawara-no-Ori-Himé herself, — the Weaving-Maiden who dwells by the shining River of Heaven.

Smiling, the aged woman turned to the fair one, who remained speechless, with downcast eyes and flushing cheeks, and said to her : —

"See, my child ! — at the moment when we could least have hoped for such a thing, the very person whom you wished to meet has come of his own accord. So fortunate a happening could have been brought about only by the will of the high gods. To think of it makes me weep for joy." And she sobbed aloud. " But now," she continued, wiping away her tears with her sleeve, " it only remains for you both — unless either prove unwilling,

152

which I doubt — to pledge yourselves to each other, and to partake of your wedding feast."

Itō answered by no word : the incomparable vision before him had numbed his will and tied his tongue. Maid-servants entered, bearing dishes and wine : the wedding feast was spread before the pair; and the pledges were given. Itō nevertheless remained as in a trance : the marvel of the adventure, and the wonder of the beauty of the bride, still bewildered him. A gladness, beyond aught that he had ever known before, filled his heart — like a great silence. But gradually he recovered his wonted calm ; and thereafter he found himself able to converse without embarrassment. Of the wine he partook freely ; and he ventured to speak, in a self-depreciating but merry way, about the doubts and fears that had oppressed him. Meanwhile the bride remained still as moonlight, never lifting her eyes, and replying only by a blush or a smile when he addressed her.

Itō said to the aged attendant : —

"Many times, in my solitary walks, I

have passed through this village without knowing of the existence of this honorable dwelling. And ever since entering here, I have been wondering why this noble household should have chosen so lonesome a place of sojourn. . . . Now that your Himégimi-Sama and I have become pledged to each other, it seems to me a strange thing that I do not yet know the name of her august family."

At this utterance, a shadow passed over the kindly face of the old woman ; and the bride, who had yet hardly spoken, turned pale, and appeared to become painfully anxious. After some moments of silence, the aged woman responded : —

"To keep our secret from you much longer would be difficult ; and I think that, under any circumstances, you should be made aware of the facts, now that you are one of us. Know then, Sir Itō, that your bride is the daughter of Shigéhira-Kyō, the great and unfortunate San-mi Chüjō."

At those words — "Shigéhira-Kyō, San-mi Chüjō" — the young samurai felt a

154

chill, as of ice, strike through all his veins. Shigéhira-Kyō, the great Héïké general and statesman, had been dust for centuries. And Itō suddenly understood that everything around him — the chamber and the lights and the banquet — was a dream of the past ; that the forms before him were not people, but shadows of people dead.

But in another instant the icy chill had passed ; and the charm returned, and seemed to deepen about him ; and he felt no fear. Though his bride had come to him out of Yomi, — out of the place of the Yellow Springs of death, — his heart had been wholly won. Who weds a ghost must become a ghost; — yet he knew himself ready to die, not once, but many times, rather than betray by word or look one thought that might bring a shadow of pain to the brow of the beautiful illusion before him. Of the affection proffered he had no misgiving : the truth had been told him when any unloving purpose might better have been served by deception. But these thoughts and emotions passed in a flash, leaving him resolved

155

to accept the strange situation as it had presented itself, and to act just as he would have done if chosen, in the years of Jü-ei, by Shigéhira's daughter.

"Ah, the pity of it!" he exclaimed; "I have heard of the cruel fate of the august Lord Shigéhira."

"Ay," responded the aged woman, sobbing as she spoke; — "it was indeed a cruel fate. His horse, you know, was killed by an arrow, and fell upon him; and when he called for help, those who had lived upon his bounty deserted him in his need. Then he was taken prisoner, and sent to Kamakura, where they treated him shamefully, and at last put him to death.[1] His wife and child — this dear maid

---

[1] Shigéhira, after a brave fight in defense of the capital, — then held by the Taïra (or Héïké) party, — was surprised and routed by Yoshitsuné, leader of the Minamoto forces. A soldier named Iyénaga, who was a skilled archer, shot down Shigéhira's horse; and Shigéhira fell under the struggling animal. He cried to an attendant to bring another horse; but the man fled. Shigéhira was then captured by Iyénaga, and eventually given up to Yoritomo, head of the Minamoto clan, who caused him to be sent in a cage to

156

here — were then in hiding; for everywhere the Héïké were being sought out and killed. When the news of the Lord Shigéhira's death reached us, the pain proved too great for the mother to bear, so the child was left with no one to care for her but me, — since her kindred had all perished or disappeared. She was only five years old. I had been her milk-nurse, and I did what I could for her. Year after year we wandered from place to place, traveling in pilgrim-garb. . . . But these tales of grief are ill-timed," exclaimed the nurse, wiping away her tears; — "pardon the foolish heart of an old woman who cannot forget the past. See! the little maid whom I fostered has now become a Himégimi-Sama indeed! — were we living in the good days of the Emperor Takakura, what a destiny might be reserved for her! However, she has obtained the husband

Kamakura. There, after sundry humiliations, he was treated for a time with consideration, — having been able, by a Chinese poem, to touch even the cruel heart of Yoritomo. But in the following year he was executed by request of the Buddhist priests of Nanto, against whom he had formerly waged war by order of Kiyomori.

whom she desired; that is the greatest happiness. . . . But the hour is late. The bridalchamber has been prepared; and I must now leave you to care for each other until morning."

She rose, and sliding back the screens parting the guest-room from the adjoining chamber, ushered them to their sleeping apartment. Then, with many words of joy and congratulation, she withdrew; and Itō was left alone with his bride.

As they reposed together, Itō said:—

"Tell me, my loved one, when was it that you first wished to have me for your husband."

(For everything appeared so real that he had almost ceased to think of the illusion woven around him.)

She answered, in a voice like a dove's voice:—

"My august lord and husband, it was at the temple of Ishiyama, where I went with my foster-mother, that I saw you for the first time. And because of seeing you, the world became changed to me from that hour and moment. But you do not remember, because our meeting was not in this, your present life : it was very, very long ago. Since that time you have passed through many deaths and births, and have had many comely bodies. But I have remained always that which you see me now : I could not obtain another body, nor enter into another state of existence, because of my great wish for you. My dear lord and husband, I have waited for you through many ages of men."

And the bridegroom felt nowise afraid at hearing these strange words, but desired nothing more in life, or in all his lives to come, than to feel her arms about him, and to hear the caress of her voice.

But the pealing of a temple-bell proclaimed the coming of dawn. Birds began to twitter; a morning breeze set all the trees a-whispering. Suddenly the old nurse pushed apart the sliding screens of the bridal-chamber, and exclaimed : —

"My children, it is time to separate ! By daylight you must not be together, even for an instant : that were fatal ! You must bid each other good-by."

Without a word, Itō made ready to depart. He vaguely understood the warning uttered, and resigned himself wholly to destiny. His will belonged to him no more ; he desired only to please his shadowy bride.

She placed in his hands a little *suzuri*, or ink-stone, curiously carved, and said : —

"My young lord and husband is a scholar; therefore this small gift will probably not be despised by him. It is of strange fashion because it is old, having been augustly bestowed upon my father by the favor of the Emperor Takakura. For that reason only, I thought it to be a precious thing."

Itō, in return, besought her to accept for a remembrance the *kōgai* [1] of his sword, which were decorated with inlaid work of silver and gold, representing plum-flowers and nightingales.

[1] This was the name given to a pair of metal rods attached to a sword-sheath, and used like chop-sticks. They were sometimes exquisitely ornamented.

Then the little *miya-dzukai* came to guide him through the garden, and his bride with her foster-mother accompanied him to the threshold.

As he turned at the foot of the steps to make his parting salute, the old woman said : —

"We shall meet again the next Year of the Boar, at the same hour of the same day of the same month that you came here. This being the Year of the Tiger, you will have to wait ten years. But, for reasons which I must not say, we shall not be able to meet again in this place; we are going to the neighborhood of Kyōto, where the good Emperor Takakura and our fathers and many of our people are dwelling. All the Héïké will be rejoiced by your coming. We shall send a *kago*[1] for you on the appointed day."

Above the village the stars were burning as Itō passed the gate; but on reaching the open road he saw the dawn brightening beyond

[1] A kind of palanquin.

leagues of silent fields. In his bosom he carried the gift of his bride. The charm of her voice lingered in his ears, — and nevertheless, had it not been for the memento which he touched with questioning fingers, he could have persuaded himself that the memories of the night were memories of sleep, and that his life still belonged to him.

But the certainty that he had doomed himself evoked no least regret : he was troubled only by the pain of separation, and the thought of the seasons that would have to pass before the illusion could be renewed for him. Ten years! — and every day of those years would seem how long! The mystery of the delay he could not hope to solve; the secret ways of the dead are known to the gods alone.

Often and often, in his solitary walks, Itō revisited the village at Kotobikiyama, vaguely hoping to obtain another glimpse of the past. But never again, by night or by day, was he able to find the rustic gate in the shadowed lane; never again could he perceive the figure of the little *miya-dzukai*, walking alone in the sunset-glow.

The village people, whom he questioned carefully, thought him bewitched. No person of rank, they said, had ever dwelt in the settlement; and there had never been, in the neighborhood, any such garden as he described. But there had once been a great Buddhist temple near the place of which he spoke; and some gravestones of the temple-cemetery were still to be seen. Itō discovered the monuments in the middle of a dense thicket. They were of an ancient Chinese form, and were covered with moss and lichens, The characters that had been cut upon them could no longer be deciphered.

Of his adventure Itō spoke to no one. But friends and kindred soon perceived a great change in his appearance and manner. Day by day he seemed to become more pale and thin, though physicians declared that he had no bodily ailment; he looked like a ghost, and moved like a shadow. Thoughtful and solitary he had always been, but now he appeared indifferent

163

to everything which had formerly given him pleasure, — even to those literary studies by means of which he might have hoped to win distinction. To his mother — who thought that marriage might quicken his former ambition, and revive his interest in life — he said that he had made a vow to marry no living woman. And the months dragged by.

At last came the Year of the Boar, and the season of autumn; but Itō could no longer take the solitary walks that he loved. He could not even rise from his bed. His life was ebbing, though none could divine the cause; and he slept so deeply and so long that his sleep was often mistaken for death.

Out of such a sleep he was startled, one bright evening, by the voice of a child; and he saw at his bedside the little *miya-dzukai* who had guided him, ten years before, to the gate of the vanished garden. She saluted him, and smiled, and said : " I am bidden to tell you that you will be received to-night at Ōhara, near Kyōto, where the new home is, and that a *kago* has been sent for you." Then she disappeared.

164

Itō knew that he was being summoned away from the light of the sun ; but the message so rejoiced him that he found strength to sit up and call his mother. To her he then for the first time related the story of his bridal, and he showed her the ink-stone which had been given him. He asked that it should be placed in his coffin, — and then he died.

The ink-stone was buried with him. But before the funeral ceremonies it was examined by experts, who said that it had been made in the period of *Jō-an* (1169 A. D.), and that it bore the seal-mark of an artist who had lived in the time of the Emperor Takakura.

STRANGER
THAN
FICTION

STRANGER
THAN
FICTION

IT was a perfect West Indian day. My friend the notary and I were crossing the island by a wonderful road which wound up through tropic forest to the clouds, and thence looped down again, through gold-green slopes of cane, and scenery amazing of violet and blue and ghost-gray peaks, to the roaring coast of the trade winds. All the morning we had been ascending, — walking after our carriage, most of the time, for the sake of the brave little mule ; — and the sea had been climbing behind us till it looked like a monstrous wall of blue, pansy-blue, under the ever heightening horizon. The heat was like the heat of a vapor-bath, but the air was good to breathe with its tropical odor, — an odor made up of smells of strange saps, queer spicy scents of mould, exhalations of aromatic decay. Moreover, the views were glimpses of Paradise; and it was a joy to watch the torrents roaring down their gorges under shadows of tree-fern and bamboo.

My friend stopped the carriage before a gateway set into a hedge full of flowers that looked like pink-and-white butterflies. " I have to make a call here," he said ; — " come in with me." We dismounted, and he knocked on the gate with the butt of his whip. Within, at the end of a shady garden, I could see the porch of a planter's house ; beyond were rows of cocoa palms, and glimpses of yellowing cane. Presently a negro, wearing only a pair of canvas trousers and a great straw hat, came hobbling to open the gate, — followed by a multitude, an astonishing multitude, of chippering chickens. Under the shadow of that huge straw hat I could not see the negro's face; but I noticed that his limbs and body were strangely shrunken, — looked as if withered to the bone. A weirder creature I had never beheld ; and I wondered at his following of chickens.

"Eh!" exclaimed the notary, "your chickens are as lively as ever! . . . I want to see Madame Floran."

"*Moin ké di*," the goblin responded huskily, in his patois; and he limped on before us, all the chickens hopping and cheeping at his withered heels.

"That fellow," my friend observed, "was bitten by a *fer-de-lance* about eight or nine years ago. He got cured, or at least half-cured, in some extraordinary way; but ever since then he has been a skeleton. See how he limps!"

The skeleton passed out of sight behind the house, and we waited a while at the front porch. Then a métisse — turbaned in wasp colors, and robed in iris colors, and wonderful to behold — came to tell us that Madame hoped we would rest ourselves in the garden, as the house was very warm. Chairs and a little table were then set for us in a shady place, and the métisse brought out lemons, sugar-syrup, a bottle of the clear plantation rum that smells like apple juice, and ice-cold water in a *dobanne* of thick red clay. My friend prepared the refreshments; and then our hostess came to greet us, and to sit with us, — a nice old lady with hair like newly minted silver. I had never seen a smile sweeter than that with which she bade us welcome; and I wondered whether she could ever have been more charming in her Creole girlhood than she now appeared, — with her kindly wrinkles, and argent hair, and frank, black, sparkling eyes. . . .

In the conversation that followed I was not able to take part, as it related only to some question of title. The notary soon arranged whatever there was to arrange; and, after some charmingly spoken words of farewell from the gentle lady, we took our departure. Again the mummified negro hobbled before us, to open the gate, — followed by all his callow rabble of chickens. As we resumed our places in the carriage we could still hear the chippering of the creatures, pursuing after that ancient scarecrow.

"Is it African sorcery?" I queried. . . . "How does he bewitch those chickens?"

" Queer — is it not ? " the notary responded as we drove away. "That negro must
now be at least eighty years old ; and he may
live for twenty years more, — the wretch ! "

The tone in which my friend uttered
this epithet — *le miserable !* — somewhat surprised me, as I knew him to be one of the kind-
liest men in the world, and singularly free from
prejudice. I suspected that a story was coming,
and I waited for it in silence.

" Listen," said the notary, after a
pause, during which we left the plantation well
behind us ; " that old sorcerer, as you call him,
was born upon the estate, a slave. The estate
belonged to M. Floran, — the husband of the
lady whom we visited ; and she was a cousin,
and the marriage was a love-match. They had
been married about two years when the revolt
occurred (fortunately there were no children),
— the black revolt of eighteen hundred and
forty-eight. Several planters were murdered ;
and M. Floran was one of the first to be killed.
And the old negro whom we saw to-day — the
old sorcerer, as you call him — left the plan-

tation, and joined the rising: do you understand?"

"Yes," I said; "but he might have done that through fear of the mob."

"Certainly: the other hands did the same. But it was he that killed M. Floran,—for no reason whatever,—cut him up with a cutlass. M. Floran was riding home when the attack was made,—about a mile below the plantation. . . . Sober, that negro would not have dared to face M. Floran: the scoundrel was drunk, of course,—raving drunk. Most of the blacks had been drinking tafia, with dead wasps in it, to give themselves courage."

"But," I interrupted, "how does it happen that the fellow is still on the Floran plantation?"

"Wait a moment! . . . When the military got control of the mob, search was made everywhere for the murderer of M. Floran; but he could not be found. He was lying out in the cane,—in M. Floran's cane!—like a field-rat, like a snake. One morning, while the gendarmes were still looking for him, he rushed

174

into the house, and threw himself down in front of Madame, weeping and screaming, ' *Aïe-yaïe-yaïe-yaïe ! — moin té tchoué y ! moin té tchoué y ! — aïe - yaïe - yaïe !* ' Those were his very words : — ' I killed him ! I killed him ! ' And he begged for mercy. When he was asked why he killed M. Floran, he cried out that it was the devil — *diabe-à* — that had made him do it ! . . . Well, Madame forgave him ! "

" But how could she ? " I queried.

" Oh, she had always been very religious," my friend responded, — " sincerely religious. She only said, ' May God pardon me as I now pardon you ! ' She made her servants hide the creature and feed him ; and they kept him hidden until the excitement was over. Then she sent him back to work ; and he has been working for her ever since. Of course he is now too old to be of any use in the field ; — he only takes care of the chickens."

" But how," I persisted, " could the relatives allow Madame to forgive him ? "

" Well, Madame insisted that he was not mentally responsible, — that he was only a

poor fool who had killed without knowing what
he was doing; and she argued that if *she* could
forgive him, others could more easily do the
same. There was a consultation; and the relatives decided so to arrange matters that Madame could have her own way."

"But why?"

"Because they knew that she found
a sort of religious consolation — a kind of religious comfort — in forgiving the wretch. She
imagined that it was her duty as a Christian,
not only to forgive him, but to take care of
him. We thought that she was mistaken, —
but we could understand. . . . Well, there is
an example of what religion can do." . . .

The suprise of a new fact, or the
sudden perception of something never before
imagined, may cause an involuntary smile. Unconsciously I smiled, while my friend was yet
speaking; and the good notary's brow dark-
ened.

"Ah, you laugh!" he exclaimed, —
"you laugh! That is wrong! — that is a mis-
176

take! . . . But you do not believe: you do not know what it is, — the true religion, — the real Christianity!"

Earnestly I made answer: —

"Pardon me! I do believe every word of what you have told me. If I laughed unthinkingly, it was only because I could not help wondering" . . .

"At what?" he questioned gravely.

"At the marvelous instinct of that negro."

"Ah, yes!" he returned approvingly. "Yes, the cunning of the animal it was, — the instinct of the brute! . . . She was the only person in the world who could have saved him."

"And he knew it," I ventured to add.

"No — no — no!" my friend emphatically dissented, — "he never could have known it! He only *felt* it! . . . Find me an instinct like that, and I will show you a brain incapable of any knowledge, any thinking, any understanding: not the mind of a man, but the brain of a beast!"

A
LETTER
FROM
JAPAN

A
LETTER
FROM
JAPAN

Tōkyō, August 1, 1904.

HERE, in this quiet suburb, where the green peace is broken only by the voices of children at play and the shrilling of cicadæ, it is difficult to imagine that, a few hundred miles away, there is being carried on one of the most tremendous wars of modern times, between armies aggregating more than half a million of men, or that, on the intervening sea, a hundred ships of war have been battling. This contest, between the mightiest of Western powers and a people that began to study Western science only within the recollection of many persons still in vigorous life, is, on one side at least, a struggle for national existence. It was inevitable, this struggle, — might perhaps have been delayed, but certainly not averted. Japan has boldly challenged an empire capable of threatening simultaneously the civilizations of the East and the West, — a mediæval power that, unless vigorously checked, seems destined to absorb Scandinavia and to dominate China. For all industrial civilization the contest is one of vast moment; — for Japan it is probably the supreme crisis in her national life. As to what her fleets and her armies have been doing, the world is fully informed; but as to what her people are doing at home, little has been written.

To inexperienced observation they would appear to be doing nothing unusual; and this strange calm is worthy of record. At the beginning of hostilities an Imperial mandate was issued, bidding all non-combatants to pursue their avocations as usual, and to trouble themselves as little as possible about exterior events; — and this command has been obeyed to the letter. It would be natural to suppose that all the sacrifices, tragedies, and uncertainties of the contest had thrown their gloom over the life of

182

the capital in especial; but there is really nothing whatever to indicate a condition of anxiety
or depression. On the contrary, one is aston-
ished by the joyous tone of public confidence,
and the admirably restrained pride of the nation
in its victories. Western tides have strewn the
coast with Japanese corpses; regiments have
been blown out of existence in the storming of
positions defended by wire-entanglements; battleships have been lost: yet at no moment has
there been the least public excitement. The
people are following their daily occupations just
as they did before the war; the cheery aspect of
things is just the same; the theatres and flower
displays are not less well patronized. The life
of Tōkyō has been, to outward seeming, hardly
more affected by the events of the war than the
life of nature beyond it, where the flowers are
blooming and the butterflies hovering as in other
summers. Except after the news of some great
victory, — celebrated with fireworks and lantern.
processions, — there are no signs of public emotion; and but for the frequent distribution of
newspaper extras, by runners ringing bells, you

could almost persuade yourself that the whole story of the war is an evil dream.

Yet there has been, of necessity, a vast amount of suffering — viewless and voiceless suffering — repressed by that sense of social and patriotic duty which is Japanese religión. As a seventeen-syllable poem of the hour tells us, the news of every victory must bring pain as well as joy : —

Gōgwai no
Tabi teki mikata
Goké ga fuè.

[*Each time that an extra is circulated the widows of foes and friends have increased in multitude.*]

The great quiet and the smiling tearlessness testify to the more than Spartan discipline of the race. Anciently the people were trained, not only to conceal their emotions, but to speak in a cheerful voice and to show a pleasant face under any stress of moral suffering; and they are obedient to that teaching to-day. It would still be thought a shame to betray per-

184

sonal sorrow for the loss of those who die for Emperor and fatherland. The public seem to view the events of the war as they would watch the scenes of a popular play. They are interested without being excited; and their extraordinary self-control is particularly shown in various manifestations of the "Play-impulse." Everywhere the theatres are producing war dramas (based upon actual fact); the newspapers and magazines are publishing war stories and novels; the cinematograph exhibits the monstrous methods of modern warfare; and numberless industries are turning out objects of art or utility designed to commemorate the Japanese triumphs.

But the present psychological condition, the cheerful and even playful tone of public feeling, can be indicated less by any general statement than by the mention of ordinary facts, — every-day matters recorded in the writer's diary.

Never before were the photographers so busy; it is said that they have not been able to fulfill half of the demands made upon them. The hundreds of thousands of men sent to the war wished to leave photographs with their families, and also to take with them portraits of parents, children, and other beloved persons. The nation was being photographed during the past six months.

A fact of sociological interest is that photography has added something new to the poetry of the domestic faith. From the time of its first introduction, photography became popular in Japan; and none of those superstitions, which inspire fear of the camera among less civilized races, offered any obstacle to the rapid development of a new industry. It is true that there exists some queer-folk beliefs about photographs, — ideas of mysterious relation between the sun-picture and the person imaged. For example: if, in the photograph of a group, one figure appear indistinct or blurred, that is thought to be an omen of sickness or death. But this superstition has its industrial value : it has compelled photographers to be careful about their work, — especially in these days of war,

186

when everybody wants to have a good clear portrait, because the portrait might be needed for another purpose than preservation in an album.

During the last twenty years there has gradually come into existence the custom of placing the photograph of a dead parent, brother, husband, or child, beside the mortuary tablet kept in the Buddhist household shrine. For this reason, also, the departing soldier wishes to leave at home a good likeness of himself.

The rites of domestic affection, in old samurai families, are not confined to the cult of the dead. On certain occasions, the picture of the absent parent, husband, brother, or betrothed, is placed in the alcove of the guest-room, and a feast laid out before it. The photograph, in such cases, is fixed upon a little stand (*dai*); and the feast is served as if the person were present. This pretty custom of preparing a meal for the absent is probably more ancient than any art of portraiture; but the modern photograph adds to the human poetry of the rite. In feudal time it was the

187

rule to set the repast facing the direction in which the absent person had gone — north, south, east, or west. After a brief interval the covers of the vessels containing the cooked food were lifted and examined. If the lacquered inner surface was thickly beaded with vapor, all was well; but if the surface was dry, that was an omen of death, a sign that the disembodied spirit had returned to absorb the essence of the offerings.

As might have been expected, in a country where the "play-impulse" is stronger, perhaps, than in any other part of the world, the Zeitgeist found manifestation in the flower displays of the year. I visited those in my neighborhood, which is the Quarter of the Gardeners. This quarter is famous for its azaleas (*tsutsuji*); and every spring the azalea gardens attract thousands of visitors, — not only by the wonderful exhibition then made of shrubs which look like solid masses of blossom (ranging up from snowy white, through all shades of pink, to a flamboyant purple) but also by displays of effigies: groups of figures ingeniously formed with living leaves and flowers. These figures, life-size, usually represent famous incidents of history or drama. In many cases — though not in all — the bodies and the costumes are composed of foliage and flowers trained to grow about a framework; while the faces, feet, and hands are represented by some kind of flesh-colored composition.

This year, however, a majority of the displays represented scenes of the war, — such as an engagement between Japanese infantry and mounted Cossacks, a night attack by torpedo boats, the sinking of a battleship. In the last-mentioned display, Russian bluejackets appeared, swimming for their lives in a rough sea; — the pasteboard waves and the swimming figures being made to rise and fall by the pulling of a string; while the crackling of quick-firing guns was imitated by a mechanism contrived with sheets of zinc.

It is said that Admiral Tōgō sent to Tōkyō for some flowering-trees in pots — inasmuch as his responsibilities allowed him no chance of seeing the cherry-flowers and the plum-blossoms in their season, — and that the gardeners responded even too generously.

Almost immediately after the beginning of hostilities, thousands of " war pictures" — mostly cheap lithographs — were published. The drawing and coloring were better than those of the prints issued at the time of the war with China ; but the details were to a great extent imaginary, — altogether imaginary as to the appearance of Russian troops. Pictures of the engagements with the Russian fleet were effective, despite some lurid exaggeration. The most startling things were pictures of Russian defeats in Korea, published before a single military engagement had taken place ; — the àrtist had " flushed to anticipate the scene." In these prints the Russians were depicted as fleeing in utter rout, leaving their officers — very fine-looking officers — dead upon the field ; while the Japanese infantry, with dreadfully determined faces, were coming up at a double. The propriety and the wisdom of thus pictorially predicting victory, and easy victory to boot, may be questioned. But I am told that the custom of so doing is an old one; and it is thought that to realize the common hope thus imaginatively is lucky. At all events, there is no attempt at deception in these pictorial undertakings;— they help to keep up the public courage, and they ought to be pleasing to the gods.

Some of the earlier pictures have now been realized in grim fact. The victories in China had been similarly foreshadowed: they amply justified the faith of the artist. . . . To-day the war pictures continue to multiply; but they have changed character. The inexorable truth of the photograph, and the sketches of the war correspondent, now bring all the vividness and violence of fact to help the artist's imagination. There was something naïve and theatrical in the drawings of anticipation; but the pictures of the hour represent the most tragic reality, — always becoming more terrible. At this writing, Japan has yet lost no single battle; but not a few of her victories have been dearly won.

To enumerate even a tenth of the various articles ornamented with designs inspired by the war — articles such as combs, clasps, fans, brooches, card-cases, purses — would require a volume. Even cakes and confectionery are stamped with naval or military designs; and the glass or paper windows of shops — not to mention the signboards — have pictures of Japanese victories painted upon them. At night the shop lanterns proclaim the pride of the nation in its fleets and armies; and a whole chapter might easily be written about the new designs in transparencies and toy lanterns. A new revolving lantern — turned by the air-current which its own flame creates — has become very popular. It represents a charge of Japanese infantry upon Russian defenses; and holes pierced in the colored paper, so as to produce a continuous vivid flashing while the transparency revolves, suggest the exploding of shells and the volleying of machine guns.

Some displays of the art-impulse, as inspired by the war, have been made in directions entirely unfamiliar to Western experience,

— in the manufacture, for example, of women's hair ornaments and dress materials. Dress goods decorated with war pictures have actually become a fashion, — especially crêpe silks for underwear, and figured silk linings for cloaks and sleeves. More remarkable than these are the new hairpins ; — by hairpins I mean those long double-pronged ornaments of flexible metal which are called *kanzashi*, and are more or less ornamented according to the age of the wearer. (The *kanzashi* made for young girls are highly decorative ; those worn by older folk are plain, or adorned only with a ball of coral or polished stone.) The new hairpins might be called commemorative : one, of which the decoration represents a British and a Japanese flag intercrossed, celebrates the Anglo-Japanese alliance ; another represents an officer's cap and sword ; and the best of all is surmounted by a tiny metal model of a battleship. The battleship-pin is not merely fantastic : it is actually pretty !

As might have been expected, military and naval subjects occupy a large place among the year's designs for toweling. The towel designs celebrating naval victories have been particularly successful : they are mostly in white, on a blue ground ; or in black, on a white ground. One of the best — blue and white — represented only a flock of gulls wheeling about the masthead of a sunken iron-clad, and, far away, the silhouettes of Japanese battleships passing to the horizon. . . . What especially struck me in this, and in several other designs, was the original manner in which the Japanese artist had seized upon the traits of the modern battleship, — the powerful and sinister lines of its shape, — just as he would have caught for us the typical character of a beetle or a lobster. The lines have been just enough exaggerated to convey, at one glance, the real impression made by the aspect of these iron monsters, — a vague impression of bulk and force and menace, very difficult to express by ordinary methods of drawing.

Besides towels decorated with artistic sketches of this sort, there have been placed upon the market many kinds of towels bearing comic war pictures, — caricatures or cartoons

which are amusing without being malignant. It
will be remembered that at the time of the first
attack made upon the Port Arthur squadron,
several of the Russian officers were in the Dalny
theatre, — never dreaming that the Japanese
would dare to strike the first blow. This inci-
dent has been made the subject of a towel design. At one end of the towel is a comic study
of the faces of the Russians, delightedly watching the gyrations of a ballet dancer. At the
other end is a study of the faces of the same
commanders when they find, on returning to
the port, only the masts of their battleships
above water. Another towel shows a procession of fish in front of a surgeon's office —
waiting their turns to be relieved of sundry bay-
onets, swords, revolvers, and rifles, which have
stuck in their throats. A third towel picture
represents a Russian diver examining, with a
prodigious magnifying-glass, the holes made
by torpedoes in the hull of a sunken cruiser.
Comic verses or legends, in cursive text, are
printed beside these pictures.

The great house of Mitsui, which

placed the best of these designs on the market, also produced some beautiful souvenirs of the war, in the shape of *fukusa*. (A *fukusa* is an ornamental silk covering, or wrapper, put over presents sent to friends on certain occasions, and returned after the present has been received.) These are made of the heaviest and costliest silk, and inclosed within appropriately decorated covers. Upon one *fukusa* is a colored picture of the cruisers Nisshin and Kasuga, under full steam; and upon another has been printed, in beautiful Chinese characters, the full text of the Imperial Declaration of war.

But the strangest things that I have seen in this line of production were silk dresses for baby girls, — figured stuffs which, when looked at from a little distance, appeared incomparably pretty, owing to the masterly juxtaposition of tints and colors. On closer inspection the charming design proved to be composed entirely of war pictures, — or, rather, fragments of pictures, blended into one astonishing combination: naval battles; burning warships; submarine mines exploding; torpedo boats attacking;

charges of Cossacks repulsed by Japanese infantry; artillery rushing into position ; storming of forts ; long lines of soldiery advancing through mist. Here were colors of blood and fire, tints of morning haze and evening glow, noon-blue and starred night-purple, sea-gray and field-green, — most wonderful thing ! . . . I suppose that the child of a military or naval officer might, without impropriety, be clad in such a robe. But then — the unspeakable pity of things !

The war toys are innumerable : I can attempt to mention only a few of the more remarkable kinds.

Japanese children play many sorts of card games, some of which are old, others quite new. There are poetical card games, for example, played with a pack of which each card bears the text of a poem, or part of a poem ; and the player should be able to remember the name of the author of any quotation in the set. Then there are geographical card games, in which each of the cards used bears the name, and perhaps a little picture, of some. famous site, town, or temple; and the player should be able to remember the district and province in which the mentioned place is situated. The latest novelty in this line is a pack of cards with pictures upon them of the Russian war vessels; and the player should be able to state what has become of every vessel named, — whether sunk, disabled, or confined in Port Arthur.

There is another card game in which the battleships, cruisers, and torpedo craft of both Japan and Russia are represented. The winner in this game destroys his "captures" by tearing the cards taken. But the shops keep packages of each class of warship cards in stock; and when all the destroyers or cruisers of one country have been put *hors de combat*, the defeated party can purchase new vessels abroad. One torpedo boat costs about one farthing; but five torpedo boats can be bought for a penny.

The toy-shops are crammed with models of battleships, — in wood, clay, porcelain, lead, and tin, — of many sizes and prices. Some of the larger ones, moved by clockwork, are named after Japanese battleships: Shikishima,

Fuji, Mikasa. One mechanical toy represents the sinking of a Russian vessel by a Japanese torpedo boat. Among cheaper things of this class is a box of colored sand, for the representation of naval engagements. Children arrange the sand so as to resemble waves; and with each box of sand are sold two fleets of tiny leaden vessels. The Japanese ships are white, and the Russian black; and explosions of torpedoes are to be figured by small cuttings of vermilion paper, planted in the sand.

The children of the poorest classes make their own war toys; and I have been wondering whether those ancient feudal laws (translated by Professor Wigmore), which fixed the cost and quality of toys to be given to children, did not help to develop that ingenuity which the little folk display. Recently I saw a group of children in our neighborhood playing at the siege of Port Arthur, with fleets improvised out of scraps of wood and some rusty nails. A tub of water represented Port Arthur. Battleships were figured by bits of plank, into which chop-sticks had been fixed to represent masts, and rolls of paper to represent funnels. Little flags, appropriately colored, were fastened to the masts with rice paste. Torpedo boats were imaged by splinters, into each of which a short thick nail had been planted to indicate a smokestack. Stationary submarine mines were represented by small squares of wood, each having one long nail driven into it; and these little things, when dropped into water with the nail-head downwards, would keep up a curious bobbing motion for a long time. Other squares of wood, having clusters of short nails driven into them, represented floating mines: and the mimic battleships were made to drag for these, with lines of thread. The pictures in the Japanese papers had doubtless helped the children to imagine the events of the war with tolerable accuracy.

Naval caps for children have become, of course, more in vogue than ever before. Some of the caps bear, in Chinese characters of burnished metal, the name of a battleship, or the words *Nippon Teikoku* (Empire of Japan),

200

— disposed like the characters upon the cap of a blue-jacket. On some caps, however, the ship's name appears in English letters, — Yashima, Fuji, etc.

The play-impulse, I had almost forgotten to say, is shared by the soldiers themselves, — though most of those called to the front do not expect to return in the body. They ask only to be remembered at the Spirit-Invoking Shrine (*Shōkonsha*), where the shades of all who die for Emperor and country are believed to gather. The men of the regiments temporarily quartered in our suburb, on their way to the war, found time to play at mimic war with the small folk of the neighborhood. (At all times Japanese soldiers are very kind to children ; and the children here march with them, join in their military songs, and correctly salute their officers, feeling sure that the gravest officer will return the salute of a little child.) When the last regiment went away, the men distributed toys among the children assembled at the station to give them a parting cheer,

— hairpins, with military symbols for ornament, to the girls; wooden infantry and tin cavalry to the boys. The oddest present was a small clay model of a Russian soldier's head, presented with the jocose promise: "If we come back, we shall bring you some real ones." In the top of the head there is a small wire loop, to which a rubber string can be attached. At the time of the war with China, little clay models of Chinese heads, with very long queues, were favorite toys.

The war has also suggested a variety of new designs for that charming object, the *toko-niwa*. Few of my readers know what a *toko-niwa*, or "alcove-garden," is. It is a miniature garden — perhaps less than two feet square — contrived within an ornamental shallow basin of porcelain or other material, and placed in the alcove of a guest-room by way of decoration. You may see there a tiny pond; a streamlet crossed by humped bridges of Chinese pattern; dwarf trees forming a grove, and shading the model of a Shinto temple; imitations in baked clay of stone lanterns, — perhaps even the appearance of a hamlet of thatched cottages. If the *toko-niwa* be not too small, you may see real fish swimming in the pond, or a pet tortoise crawling among the rockwork. Sometimes the miniature garden represents Hōrai, and the palace of the Dragon-King.

Two new varieties have come into fashion. One is a model of Port Arthur, showing the harbor and the forts ; and with the materials for the display there is sold a little map, showing how to place certain tiny battleships, representing the imprisoned and the investing fleets. The other *toko-niwa* represents a Korean or Chinese landscape, with hill ranges and rivers and woods ; and the appearance of a battle is created by masses of toy soldiers — cavalry, infantry, and artillery — in all positions of attack and defense. Minute forts of baked clay, bristling with cannon about the size of small pins, occupy elevated positions. When properly arranged the effect is panoramic. The soldiers in the foreground are about an inch long ; those a little farther away about half as long; and those upon the hills are no larger than flies.

But the most remarkable novelty of this sort yet produced is a kind of *toko-niwa* recently on display at a famous shop in Ginza. A label bearing the inscription, *Kaï-téï no Ikken* (View of the Ocean-Bed) sufficiently explained the design. The *suïbon*, or "water-tray," containing the display was half filled with rocks and sand so as to resemble a sea-bottom; and little fishes appeared swarming in the foreground. A little farther back, upon an elevation, stood Otohimé, the Dragon-King's daughter, surrounded by her maiden attendants, and gazing, with just the shadow of a smile, at two men in naval uniform who were shaking hands, — dead heroes of the war: Admiral Makaroff and Commander Hirosé! . . . These had esteemed each other in life; and it was a happy thought thus to represent their friendly meeting in the world of Spirits.

Though his name is perhaps unfamiliar to English readers, Commander Takeo Hirosé has become, deservedly, one of Japan's national heroes. On the 27th of March, during the second attempt made to block the entrance to Port Arthur, he was killed while endeavoring to help a comrade, — a comrade who had formerly saved him from death. For five years Hirosé had been a naval attaché at St. Petersburg, and had made many friends in Russian naval and military circles. From boyhood his life had been devoted to study and duty ; and it was commonly said of him that he had no particle of selfishness in his nature. Unlike most of his brother officers, he remained unmarried, — holding that no man who might be called on at any moment to lay down his life for his country had a moral right to marry. The only amusements in which he was ever known to indulge were physical exercises ; and he was acknowledged one of the best *jūjutsu* (wrestlers) in the empire. The heroism of his death, at the age of thirty-six, had much less to do with the honors paid to his memory than the self-denying heroism of his life.

Now his picture is in thousands of

homes, and his name is celebrated in every village. It is celebrated also by the manufacture of various souvenirs, which are sold by myriads. For example, there is a new fashion in sleeve-buttons, called *Kinen-botan*, or " Commemoration-buttons." Each button bears a miniature portrait of the commander, with the inscription, *Shichi-shō hōkoku*, " Even in seven successive lives — for love of country." It is recorded that Hirosé often cited, to friends who criticised his ascetic devotion to duty, the famous utterance of Kusunoki Masashigé, who declared, ere laying down his life for the Emperor Go-Daigo, that he desired to die for his sovereign in seven successive existences.

But the highest honor paid to the memory of Hirosé is of a sort now possible only in the East, though once possible also in the West, when the Greek or Roman patriot-hero might be raised, by the common love of his people, to the place of the Immortals. . . . Wine-cups of porcelain have been made, decorated with his portrait ; and beneath the portrait appears, in ideographs of gold, the inscription,

206

Gunshin Hirosé Chūsa. The character "gun" signifies war; the character "*shin,*" a god, — either in the sense of *divus* or *deus*, according to circumstances; and the Chinese text, read in the Japanese way, is *Ikusa no Kami.* Whether that stern and valiant spirit is really invoked by the millions who believe that no brave soul is doomed to extinction, no well-spent life laid down in vain, no heroism cast away, I do not know. But, in any event, human affection and gratitude can go no farther than this; and it must be confessed that Old Japan is still able to confer honors worth dying for.

Boys and girls in all the children's schools are now singing the Song of Hirosé Chūsa, which is a marching song. The words and the music are published in a little booklet, with a portrait of the late commander upon the cover. Everywhere, and at all hours of the day, one hears this song being sung : —

He whose every word and deed gave to men an example of what the war-folk of the

207

Empire of Nippon should be, — Commander Hirosé: is he really dead?

Though the body die, the spirit dies not. He who wished to be reborn seven times into this world, for the sake of serving his country, for the sake of requiting the Imperial favor, — Commander Hirosé: has he really died?

" Since I am a son of the Country of the Gods, the fire of the evil-hearted Russians cannot touch me !" — The sturdy Takeo who spoke thus: can he really be dead? . . .

Nay ! that glorious war-death meant undying fame ; —beyond a thousand years the valiant heart shall live ; — as to a god of war shall reverence be paid to him. . . .

Observing the playful confidence of this wonderful people in their struggle for existence against the mightiest power of the West, — their perfect trust in the wisdom of their leaders and the valor of their armies, — the good humor of their irony when mocking the enemy's blunders, — their strange capacity to find, in the world-stirring events of the hour, the same amusement that they would find in watching a melodrama, — one is tempted to ask: "What would be the moral consequence of a national defeat?" . . . It would depend, I think, upon circumstances. Were Kuropatkin able to fulfill his rash threat of invading Japan, the nation would probably rise as one man. But otherwise the knowledge of any great disaster would be bravely borne. From time unknown Japan has been a land of cataclysms, — earthquakes that ruin cities in the space of a moment; tidal waves, two hundred miles long, sweeping whole coast populations out of existence; floods submerging hundreds of leagues of well-tilled fields; eruptions burying provinces. Calamities like this have disciplined the race in resignation and in patience; and it has been well trained also to bear with courage all the misfortunes of war. Even by the foreign peoples that have been most closely in contact with her, the capacities of Japan remained unguessed. Perhaps her power to resist aggression is far surpassed by her power to endure.

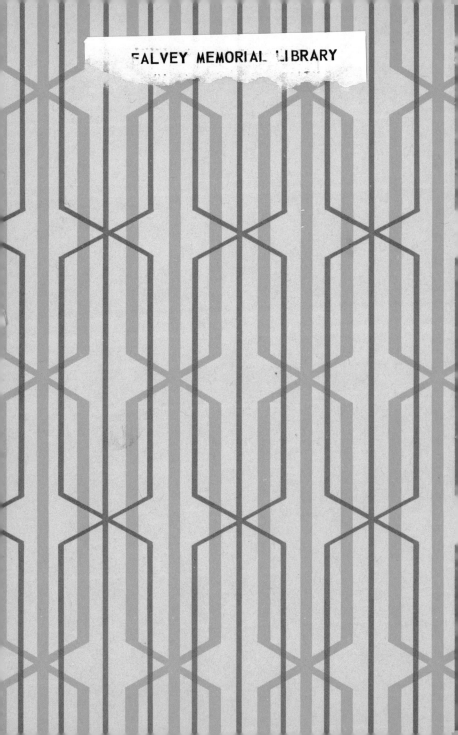